PENGUIN BOOKS

THE DANCE OF DEATH

Manna Bahadur is a novelist, poet and media professional. Her works include *Neelanjana*, a novel, published in 2007 and *Aks Mere Jazbaat Ke*, a book of poems, geet and ghazals, published in 2006. She lives in Faridabad.

MANNA BAHADUR

THE DANCE OF DEATH

Penguin
metro reads

An imprint of Penguin Random House

METRO READS

USA | Canada | UK | Ireland | Australia
New Zealand | India | South Africa | China | Singapore

Metro Reads is part of the Penguin Random House group of companies
whose addresses can be found at global.penguinrandomhouse.com

Published by Penguin Random House India Pvt. Ltd
4th Floor, Capital Tower 1, MG Road,
Gurugram 122 002, Haryana, India

Penguin
Random House
India

First published by Penguin Books India 2012

ISBN 9780143067009

Typeset in Goudy by R. Ajith Kumar, New Delhi
Printed at Repro India Limited

www.penguin.co.in

MIX
Paper from
responsible sources
FSC® C047271

This is a legitimate digitally printed version of the book and therefore might not
have certain extra finishing on the cover.

1

21 June 1976. 6.30 p.m.

Dismay was written large on Meera's face. She was finding her husband's indifference both exasperating and disturbing. It was definitely an unprecedented situation in the life of Justice Shankar and his wife Meera. Meera was proud of the thirty-five years their marriage had endured with only the occasional differences in opinion and some inconsequential spats. Meera thanked god for that and for the fact that between the two of them there had always been an easy and honest communication. They never kept secrets from each other, and trust was their rock. Then how was it that Justice Shankar was hiding this letter from her? Meera had asked him twice about it, but he had avoided her gaze and responded, 'Oh! It's nothing important.'

'Who is it from?' Meera persisted.

The judge, her husband, did not answer.

'Show me!' Meera extended her hand.

Shankar tried to make light of the situation. 'You remember the girlfriend I told you about, the one I had in kindergarten? She's written to me and has asked me not to show the letter to anyone!' Meera was not amused and did not withdraw her outstretched hands, still asking to see the letter. At this Shankar abruptly got up, put the letter back in the envelope, and said, 'I told you it is nothing! Its just one of those . . . it concerns my office and a case . . .' Before Meera could probe further, he put the envelope in his pocket and headed for the office room just next to the veranda where this disagreeable little exchange had taken place.

Meera was put off. Since when had this need to hide office matters from her arisen? Especially when they had always shared and discussed interesting case histories. The secrecy unnerved Meera.

The weather, too, was ideal for snapping at one another. The evening, in the middle of the summer in Patna, was sticky, humid and altogether unpleasant. All humour in their lives had suddenly just sunk with the setting sun. Justice Shankar was in no mood to relent and an immensely upset Meera felt like reminding her husband about her right to information. She kept wondering what was so special about the letter that it could create such unpleasantness between them. Meera was convinced something was wrong and she was determined to find out what it was.

The couple had been living in a huge bungalow on Strand Road for the past five years. The house was one of those majestic living quarters allotted to High Court judges or very senior government officials. Beautiful laburnum and gulmohar trees lined the Strand Road, one of the prime areas of the capital of Bihar. The area was so green with tall neem and peepal trees that the evening temperature in this part of town was lower than the rest of Patna. The British had had these rows of fabulous, palatial bungalows built on the Strand Road, and the area around the Rajbhawan for their senior officers. Each compound was spread over more than five acres, with tennis courts, landscaped, rolling lawns, vegetable gardens and a large barrack of rooms to house their personal staff. Each bungalow itself was double-storeyed with an en suite bedroom, a large drawing room, dining hall and an office, with an attached secretary's cabin, on the ground floor. Four huge bedrooms with balconies and a deep triangular veranda made up the first floor.

The ground floor patio was more like their living room. This was where the family spent most of their time together. They had their morning and evening tea here and it was the general sit-out area, with cushioned cane chairs amidst pots of healthy green plants. This was also where the Shankars were having their evening tea when the letter arrived and created a ripple in their happy, placid lives. Meera, tall and elegant, was always impeccably dressed in cool and crisply starched cotton saris. Justice Shankar, in spite of his thinning grey hair, looked handsome with his stylish spectacles and

sharp features. He sang beautifully, and he thought he had
impressed Meera with his romantic songs during college
days, only to realize later that Meera was tone deaf. The
mutual attraction and love had endured, undimmed, these
many years. However, after so many years spent together,
one does make allowances for occasional idiosyncrasies.
So, in keeping with their daily routine, Meera got up and
joined Justice Shankar in the lawns for the evening stroll.
As they neared the main gate, the armed guards standing
there clicked their heels and sharply saluted. Justice Shankar
was presiding over the ongoing criminal case against Daataa
Anand, the founder of a religious sect, and the government
had thought fit to provide special, round-the-clock security
for him and his family.

Shankar, on the other hand, had not asked for protection
and was very unhappy about this. He suspected that the
security guards had been installed mainly to spy on him.
His reasons were valid, too. It was the time of the state-
imposed Emergency. Justice Shankar, a strong, upright public
servant, had taken a stance against the Emergency. He had
gone against government orders and fearlessly awarded bail
to a number of young students who had been put behind
bars merely for raising their voices against the Emergency
and the injustice spreading in the society as a result of it.
The air outside the jails where the students were held had
reverberated with full-throated slogans—'Justice Shankar
ki jai!' The students were overwhelmed by the thought that
a government servant in these times, and a judge, no less,
could be as fair and courageous as Shankar. They had all

made up their minds to support him all the way in case he was made to suffer the consequences of his judgement. These were precarious times. To go against the government, which was embodied by the supreme leader, was to be blacklisted. However, Justice Shankar was not bothered. He was a firm believer in god and maintained that the lord always favours those who tread the path of truth and justice. No matter what happened, he would not give up his power to make decisions based on justice, fairness and logic and never yield to the unfair, imbalanced, egoistical demands of any one person in the name of the Emergency!

Late that night, after Justice Shankar had gone off to sleep, the telephone rang. The servants had all retired to their respective quarters so Meera got up to take the call. The telephone lying in the dining room was not working and the other one was kept in the office room. By the time Meera reached, it stopped ringing. Meera was about to switch on the lights when she saw one of the guards peeping in through the window. She was startled and got a little scared to see his face pressing against the window when the phone abruptly rang again. As she looked out apprehensively again after a few seconds, she was relieved that the guard wasn't at the window. She turned her attention to the ringing telephone— it was emitting long single beeps that normally signalled an STD call. It could be her daughter calling up from Delhi. She picked up the receiver, looking out of the window. She did not say a word, fearing that this was one of those crank calls they had been receiving lately. Her daughter Mona spoke, 'Hello? Is anybody there?'

Immediately relieved, Meera answered, 'Yes baby, I am awake. How come you are calling so late? It's close to midnight!'

'I don't know, Amma . . .' There was hesitation in her voice. 'I was feeling very uneasy. Are you and Babuji all right?'

'Of course, beta, what will happen to us? We have these armed guards to watch the house and the entire compound and then god almighty, too, is with us. So just don't worry.'

'I don't know, Amma, but somehow I have this nagging feeling that things are not all right. Since the day this Daataa Anand's case has come up for hearing in Babuji's court, I feel very scared.'

'It's nothing, beta, such cases keep coming.' Meera was trying to reassure her daughter even though she wasn't herself completely convinced about what she was saying.

'I know, but the newspapers keep reporting on Daataa Anand and he seems like a very dangerous man. Apparently, he is the founder and head of a religious sect with a vast following. The sect he runs is one of tantriks who do all sorts of black magic. One report even said that they dance with this long trishul in their hands, play with skulls and bones, and do all sorts of scary things. I only hope that they will not harm our family even if the judgement goes against them. They look like they can harm . . .'

'Have faith. Nothing will happen!' Meera interrupted her, 'Your babuji has never harmed anyone, so nobody will harm him and his family. Relax.' Then, changing the topic of discussion, she asked, 'How are you all? Is Sandeep all right?' Sandeep was their grandson.

Mona answered mostly in monosyllabic 'hmms' and 'haans' and then hung up. But she *was* very scared and the reason for her fright was her son. Like the one time last week, when she had arrived just in time to prevent seven-year-old Sandeep from giving their personal details away on the phone. It had happened thus—when the phone rang, Sandeep picked it up and began talking. Mona heard all this from the other room and smiled, relieved that Sandeep had started early, making friends and easily talking to them on the phone. But when she came close and heard the conversation, she panicked. Sandeep was informing the caller about his school—Delhi Public School, that he was in class two and that he took the school bus. Just as he was about to give the route number to the person at the other end, Mona snatched the phone from his hands. She heard a male voice say, 'Yes . . . yes, say it beta, your route number is . . .'

Mona asked, 'Who are you?'

She heard loud laughter, then the phone was disconnected.

Of late, these strange calls had become frequent. But whenever she or her husband picked up the telephone, nobody said anything. They would hear odd laughter and then a sort of a strange crying, a bit like a howling dog. This was the second time that Sandeep had picked up the phone and these people were asking him the same set of questions, trying to find out his school's name, bus route number and the school timings. And Mona was very sure that this had something to do with the Daataa Anand case her father was handling.

She kept thinking the whole day if she should tell her

mother about it and had finally picked up the telephone to inform her. But when she heard her mother's sleepy voice, she decided against it. There was no reason for her mother to get worked up and lose sleep. At her age, and with a high blood pressure problem, this was uncalled for.

While talking to Mona on the phone, Meera rummaged through her husband's drawers in the office table and found the letter he had been hiding from her in the evening. The office window had light curtains and she did not want the security chaps watching her from outside, so she did not turn on the lights. She went to the dining hall, switched on the lamp in the corner, and opened the envelope. She unfolded the letter. One look and she nearly passed out.

A set of ghastly pictures had been drawn on plain paper in red ink. They were crude representations of Meera's daughter and sons and several drops of the blood-like red ink were gruesomely splattered all over the page. No wonder, then, that her husband had not wanted her to see the letter!

Meera swayed for a moment. She managed to catch hold of a chair and slumped down. Her head was reeling, her mouth was dry. She was shivering with fright. She sat motionless for some time. When she came to her senses, she realized how right her husband had been in not showing the letter to her. She now respected him even more for shielding her from such cruelties, but she also grew determined to help him. She shuddered at the thought of the torture he must have gone through.

The big problem now was that her husband was not supposed to know that she had seen the letter. She couldn't talk to him about it and she would have to keep it a complete secret from the rest of the world.

She soon understood why Mona had been so afraid—her daughter saw much more than her. Mona would have to be alerted and steps would need to be taken to protect her and her family. What had the world come to! People were terrorizing innocents to protect the criminals. Should she inform the police? But how helpful would the police be? Besides, her husband knew better—he would have sought their help had he thought that to be the right approach. Meera began earnestly praying with folded hands even as tears rolled down her cheeks: 'Dear god, please protect my family. Please save them from these merciless criminals who pose as your devotees!'

2

In 1976 Patna was a laidback city, even though it was the capital of the populous state of Bihar. Residents had ample time on their hands and nothing much to do. Any occasion for excitement was keenly welcomed and for this reason the news was followed with interest. But this was before the days of cable TV and Doordarshan was the only the channel on TV. And lately, Doordarshan had been rather fixated on the super achievements of the incumbent government. It was little wonder, then, that the entire city had gathered to hear the proceedings of the criminal case against the notorious Daataa Anand. The courtroom was overflowing and a large number of fascinated onlookers had spilled out on the lawns too.

Kishen Das, a second-year student of Patna College, was reluctant to accompany his fellow students to the High

Court. He would rather play a game of badminton in the college premises or meet his girlfriend, the petite and pretty Seema. If she was busy with her classes, he would go to the bookshop, buy a thriller or a mystery, and wait for her while reading the book at the gates of the Patna Women's College where Seema studied.

Kishen was a student of economics so court cases and legal matters did not interest him at all. But his friends would not listen to his pleas. They dragged him along. He had no choice but to follow them disinterestedly. He planned to quietly disappear from there at an opportune moment. The court corridors were buzzing with tales of Daataa Anand. Kishen was quietly standing in the corridors when he overheard this interesting bit of conversation: '. . . and he wants to conquer life and death, just imagine!' Kishen turned around to see a few men huddled together. He really had nothing better to do, so he edged closer. He caught the last bit of a sentence, '. . . conquer life and death? Is he god?'

'And have you heard about his dream?' a man interjected.

'What dream?'

'The story is that goddess Kali has blessed him. Apparently she came to him in a dream and said that soon Daataa would be worshipped by people for his supernatural powers, people would queue up with dead bodies of their dear ones, and he would be able to resurrect them.'

'Really? Can that happen? Wouldn't that be great?'

'All bullshit! Have you heard about what goes on in his ashram?'

'Yes! Yes! Who doesn't know about that! The young

misses . . . the hot kisses . . . and the feel-each-other dances. Shameful! They are all immoral sinners . . .'

'Sinners? Nonsense . . .' chuckled another. 'I was keen to join them a few years ago when my wife, along with the children was going to her parents for the summer . . .'

'Then why didn't you?'

'You know my wife,' he whined. 'She thought I looked very happy at the thought of her going away and promptly decided to stay back!' There was a loud burst of laughter from the group.

Kishen Das smiled. He was enjoying the conversation when a man brushed past him. Suddenly Kishen had a queer sensation. He felt as if he had received an electric shock. He was dizzy for a split second. When he looked behind him, he saw a saffron-robed figure of medium height and medium build hurriedly passing by.

The group talking about Daataa Anand till now suddenly fell silent. Nudging each other, they asked, 'Isn't he Daataa Anand?'.

Kishen looked back again, but by now the man had gone ahead. He seemed to be in a tearing hurry. Kishen's interest was suddenly aroused. An urge to see Daataa Anand overpowered him. He wanted to see the man who, according to the gossips in the corridor, could bring the dead back to life. Was that true, or even possible? He felt a strange force drawing him towards Daataa; a magnetic pull he could not resist. He soon found himself sitting on the last benches of the courtroom, almost in spite of himself, his eyes staring fixedly at Daataa Anand. And, to his keen surprise, the overriding emotion that he felt for that man in saffron was a vicious hatred.

Kishen felt unable to analyse his own reactions. He knew his feelings to be immature, irrational and baseless and he had no idea how it was that he could feel so strongly about a man whom he did not know and had never met. Just half an hour ago he knew nothing about Daataa Anand or the case against him. Yet here he was, convinced that the man was a master criminal for whom the worst punishment, even the death sentence, would be insufficient. Kishen remained disturbed and restless the whole day. He was unable to sleep properly that night, tossing and turning till the late hours. And when he finally went to sleep, nightmares gripped him. He saw that a saffron-clad monster was twisting his neck. Choking and suffocated, he stood up, even as he was asleep, and began running helter skelter around his bed, gasping for breath. Kishen's father heard the commotion and came to his room. He shook Kishen awake. When he came to senses, Kishen found himself lying on the floor with his neck twisted and stiff and his whole body soaked in perspiration.

3

Having lost his case in the lower court, Daataa had appealed to the High Court. There was not much hope of his winning there too, but that did not deter him from trying his luck. The public had full faith that the police had established a foolproof case with eyewitnesses and concrete evidence, but Daataa was determined to prove his innocence. The headline, 'Hopes Recede for Daataa' did not affect his mental toughness. On the contrary, he rustled up an unwavering resolution to stick to his guns.

The people who were discussing the details of the case pronounced gravely on what Daataa Anand's fate should be—should he be hanged, or imprisoned for life? Each group had their own reasons. However, both groups were united on one point: Daataa Anand richly deserved whatever fate was to befall him.

There was a third set of people, Daataa's followers, who believed equally strongly that their dharma guru, the leader of their religious sect, had done nothing wrong. In fact, he could do no wrong. They felt that it was only the non-believers who were jealous of Daataa's fame and following. However, it was difficult for non-believers to understand and accept Daataa's spiritual superiority over others. They were scared of the kind of power that they had heard he wanted to acquire with practice, meditation and his occult experiments.

It was not just a section of the general public that did not trust Daataa Anand. He had actually begun his activities in West Bengal where he had gained a considerable following. The Communist regime in power in the state at that time looked at Daataa with a suspicious eye—he was getting too popular with the masses. According to the Communist regime, what Daataa Anand was preaching was sheer madness, it would corrode the health of society, and it would poison the roots of growth. When the state government began to make life uncomfortable for the guru, he crossed, along with his followers, into Patna. The Emergency-wielding central government, too, was inclined to view the religious guru and his sect with a degree of wariness. The party supremo, Indira Gandhi, was not prepared to tolerate anyone who derived power from popularity amongst the general public. She felt threatened by such people. She suspected these gurus, under the garb of their religious teachings, of inciting the public against her. She had been prepared to take whatever steps it took to wipe Daataa Anand out and it was fortuitous that the situation had taken care of itself without her having to take any steps. Daataa was now declared a criminal, and she need not worry about him.

Daataa Anand's followers pitied those who did not understand or appreciate him. Such people were, according to them, ignorant fools, illiterate, not aware of their higher self, and did not know what they were missing! According to them, they just needed to come close to Daataa once to have that enriching experience of everlasting bliss and tranquillity; to understand life, to realize their own being, to swim in the ocean of happiness! How unfortunate were they who doubted and pointed fingers at Daataa, god forgive them their folly. They didn't know what they were doing, and what they were missing. Daataa Anand's followers then picked up the ritual skull and trishul, the jhaal and manjira, and began dancing and singing with gay abandon:

Anandam hi anandam, de anandam le anandam
Daataa bole kshanik janam, anandam hi anandam.

4

Newspaper journalists, some even from overseas—for Daataa Anand had followers abroad as well—were in full attendance at the Patna High Court to cover the sensational story. They were alert, looking all around with great interest so as not miss out anything. There weren't multiple news channels then like there are today. There was just one, Doordarshan, and it was a government-controlled mouthpiece. The channel enjoyed carte blanche monopoly. People had to see and believe what the channel wanted them to see and believe. For them the only important face, news and reality was Mrs Indira Gandhi's. Doordarshan survived just for her. The news began and ended with her name.

In such an atmosphere, was it any surprise that Doordarshan wasn't interested at all in Daataa Anand? Any number of new religious leaders were burgeoning all over, so why should Doordarshan waste its footage over them? And then, of course, there was the 'father' of Doordarshan: the information and broadcasting ministry, the self-appointed moral guardian of the public. The ministry felt that it would be unwise to telecast the ghastly trial of Daataa Anand. It was not good for public consumption. The vulnerable, impressionable minds of the public must not be exposed to the wicked ways of a religious guru! So what need was there for a team to be sent to Patna? When the judgement would be finally delivered, it could simply be read out in a dry and matter-of-fact manner minus any picture or embellishments on the national news. Doordarshan and the information and broadcasting ministry naïvely believed that only people who lived in and around Patna knew of Daataa Anand, and contrived to keep the rest of the country and the world thinking that everything was running smoothly and efficiently.

Daataa Anand was no ordinary man. His real name was Anurag Kumar Chowdhury, and he was reported to have killed or to have been involved in the murder of ten people, most of them his own close disciples. The police had information about his nefarious activities, but Daataa had managed to outsmart them. But this time the police swooped in so suddenly that the guru had no time to cook up a convincing story. He made lame excuses, cried and pleaded, but the officer had seen it all happen in front of him. Daataa was dumped at the back of the police jeep that raced to the police station with the prize catch. Daataa kept wondering who could have the guts to breach his trust and inform the police? Much to his shock, it turned out that his bête noire was a woman named Rachna, who claimed to be Daataa's wife. It was a different matter that nobody had ever seen her with him, nor was there any evidence of her living in Daataa's ashram. Whatever the intricacies of their relationship, the fact remained that all the information she provided to the police regarding Daataa Anand turned out to be correct. However, after the incident, she went missing and the police had been unable to trace her.

Some key questions remained: were Daataa's devotees killed one by one within a period of ten months or had they committed suicide? If they had committed suicide, why was it that so many of them had chosen to do it? And if they were killed, who was responsible for the murders? And to these questions was added one crucial point: why would Daataa Anand become tense and speechless every time Rachna's name was mentioned? Was she really his wife? And if not, then who was she? How did she wield such mesmerizing power over him? Where had she disappeared? Had she been kidnapped and hidden or had she been killed?

There was another bizarre twist to the case. All the three judges who had earlier heard the case had met with very peculiar fates. The first judge suffered a massive heart attack even as the case had opened in his courtroom. The second one became a victim of a car accident. The third one had suffered such deep depression that he resigned from his post and migrated to California to live with his son.

This case had been dragging in the courts for almost a decade without any conclusion in sight. And the big question on everyone's minds was this: how would Justice Shankar handle it? Would he be strong enough to take the pressure—human or divine—or crumble like the previous judges?

On the other hand, Daataa's supporters maintained that their guru had taught others to love humanity. He preached that to attain supreme bliss and happiness, one has to love and respect one's fellow beings. He advocated patience and tolerance towards all creatures of god. What had provoked him then and brought about such intense hatred that he stooped to killing? Murdering ten human beings, like a serial killer? What could be his motive? Could he be suffering from a split personality? The murderous instinct was in direct contrast to his gentle, charming and religious nature.

Before all these murders came to light, there had been another surreptitious rumour—two men had forcefully entered Daataa's bedroom and assaulted him. They were about to kill him when his guards charged in and saved the guru.

The media, in those days, was not as alert and powerful as it is today. This particular incident never became public and remained a rumour. People gathered random information and put two and two together. It was alleged that these two men had come to take revenge for the rape and assault of their wives and daughters. This conclusion, however, was dismissed as rubbish by the guru's disciples. Daataa was a religious and god-fearing person; somebody was just trying to malign his image.

But soon after all this happened, Daataa Anand was caught in mysterious, compromising circumstances from the jungles near Hazaribagh. Doubts then began to resurface. Was there some truth, after all, in the previous allegations? Daataa's innocent and soft-spoken persona made it extremely difficult for people to believe that he could harbour any killer streak, but certain undeniable facts seemed to be saying otherwise.

5

The telephone was ringing in Justice Shankar's chamber, but he ignored it. He had stopped picking it up since the day someone tried to threaten him over the phone. His family, relatives and people close to him had devised a signal. When they called, they would let the phone ring thrice, disconnect and call again. But this time, obviously, it was from somebody unknown. It was still ringing when Justice Mukherjee entered Justice Shankar's large teak-panelled chamber, with high ceilings and a plush wall-to-wall carpet in wine red, a rotating bookshelf stuffed with legal reference books standing on the right of the judge's high chair and a dial-up telephone sitting on the left of his table. Mukherjee looked at the phone and chuckled, 'This can only be my peon ringing up. I had asked him to check if you have arrived. And now that stupid idiot, even if he sees us here together, will not disconnect unless somebody tells him to. He is an absolute fool! Don't know how he was appointed!' Justice Shankar always enjoyed how Justice Mukherjee stayed in a perennial bad mood. He replied laughingly. 'Interview and selection of the best, sir!' Justice Mukherjee was not offended. He knew Justice Shankar too well, and expected and enjoyed such retorts. He sometimes even envied his quick repartee. He recalled how, when a case was once announced in the court, 'The Bihar government versus Mrs Veena Varma, wife of Mr G.K. Varma and others.' Justice Shankar promptly quipped, 'Oh really! Which others?' Traditionally, a junior judge goes to the senior's chamber and from there they both head to court. So, as soon as Justice Mukherjee came to Justice Shankar's chamber, the two walked down the corridor towards the courtroom. They were escorted by peons in their impressive uniforms. Justice Shankar disliked these British traditions: it harked back to their colonial origins, he thought. Some day, he thought, he would definitely raise his voice against it.

As they were proceeding, Justice Mukherjee tried to make conversation. He asked Justice Shankar if he also felt that this hardcore criminal Daataa Anand had committed so many murders in order to save himself from some very grave, uncomfortable truth—or could there be a woman behind all this? Perhaps it had something to do with a huge amount of money, or perhaps some treasure? He wondered aloud about who exactly Daataa was. He was known to have good foreign connections, too.

'I hope he is not running an international spy network! Could be a traitor also, who knows?' he said aloud.

When he saw Justice Shankar glaring at him, he added

very confidently, 'No, no, anything is possible, isn't it?' He spoke in his typical Bengali accent. 'Such maarciless people like him don't even need a reason. Killing is in their blaad, you know!'

Justice Shankar did not respond to such statements. There was a difference between his and Justice Mukherjee's way of thinking. Justice Shankar believed that nobody should be called a criminal until his crime is proved. Whereas, Justice Mukherjee, if he could have had his way, would award the severest punishment to the suspect without even hearing the case.

'If the police had caught him red-handed then where was the need for an argument? No, no, these arguments unnecessarily caamplicate the matter,' he was saying, absolutely sure of his logic.

The peon standing at the door announced the arrival of the bench—Justice Shankar and Justice Mukherjee. As soon as they entered, everybody stood up. Thereafter, the court proceedings began. The counsel for defence stood up and his arguments started.

'Yes, my lord, it is true that Daataa was caught from the same spot where the unfortunate man Rakesh committed suicide by immolating himself.'

The judge quipped, 'The report filed by the superintendent of police says that when he reached the spot, he found Daataa dancing around the fire with a dead body in his hands.'

'As it was late in the evening, the SP made a visual error, my lord! It was not a dead body that he saw, but a blanket in the hands of Daataa Anand with which he was trying to douse the fire,' the counsel for defence confidently replied.

'All right, that means Daataa had prior knowledge of Rakesh intending to commit suicide by setting himself on fire, and therefore, he had gone there well prepared with a blanket.' Justice Shankar said cuttingly.

The counsel for defence rose. 'Daataa was informed by another disciple that Rakesh had been extremely depressed since his last visit to the doctor. When Daataa asked to see Rakesh, it was found that he had been missing. He deputed ten of his disciples immediately for a search operation. The holy, noble soul that he was, he was so concerned and worried—Rakesh was one of Daataa's favourite disciples too. He could not hold himself back any longer—he simply rushed out and frantically started searching for Rakesh. It was then that he saw the fire in the jungle. He picked up his own blanket lying in his car and tried to reach there quickly, cutting through thorns and bushes, not caring for his own safety, and tried to save the poor man. However, it was too late. Then suddenly, the police arrived, and without trying to find the truth, arrested him.'

'How are such things happening only to Daataa's "favourite" disciples?' The judge put special emphasis on the word 'favourite'.

'Simply unfortunate, my lord! God's will is beyond human comprehension,' replied the lawyer coolly.

'The place of immolation—isn't it about 180 kilometres away from his ashram?' enquired Justice Shankar, looking at his file.

'It's 176 kilometres to be precise, my lord!' corrected the defence advocate for Daataa.

'Interesting! And Daataa managed to reach there well on time to douse the fire, ready and prepared with a blanket in his car?' the judge questioned sharply.

'No, my lord, how could he cover 176 kilometres, and reach the spot well on time to extinguish the fire? It is not possible.' The well-prepared lawyer smiled and added, 'My esteemed client, Daataa Anand, happened to be on his way to visit his mother in Hazaribagh. He had halted at one of his ashrams on the way. Rakesh was travelling along with him too, in another car. Daataa was told about Rakesh at about 6 p.m. when he called his disciples for a meeting. The jungle where the unfortunate suicide took place was hardly four kilometres away from that particular ashram. There were no motorable roads to the jungle—that is why Daataa had to walk to the spot. He managed to reach there only by 7.30, after hunting for him in all other directions.'

'And the police arrived there at 7.45 p.m., and promptly arrested Daataa Anand. Wonderful! You mean to say that Rachna, his wife, informed the police at 3 p.m., of the impending danger to Rakesh's life? She was not even living in his ashram and yet she had all the details; whereas the father figure of all his followers, Daataa Anand, was blissfully unaware of it till 6 p.m.?' asked Justice Shankar.

'Unfortunately that is true, my lord! How and what she informed the police is a mystery for us, too. However, the point to be noted, my lord, is that Rachna's claim to be my client's wife is not true. My client has denied any such relationship with her. He has no knowledge of this woman. He has never met or seen Rachna.'

Justice Shankar was not convinced. He noticed the sudden nervous twitch on Daataa Anand's face as he consciously tried to avoid eye contact with the judge when Rachna's name was mentioned. He made a few notes in his file and thought that it would be interesting to unravel the truth.

Justice Mukherjee looked at Justice Shankar sitting on his right in the courtroom and smiled cynically. His expressions were transparent. It was obvious what he thought: 'Justice Shankar, what did I tell you? I never had any doubts that Daataa Anand was the killer. Caught red-handed from the scene of the crime! What more do you want? The lawyer is unnecessarily complicating the issue, telling lies. There is no need to waste the court's precious time—just sign the verdict "guilty" and let us close this case.'

Kishen Das was sitting on the last bench as always, listening in rapt attention. He had developed an unexplainable interest in this case and he never failed to turn up for the hearings. He was not a disciple of Daataa Anand's, had nothing to do with this trial, law was not even his subject at college, he had no fascination for lawyers, court or judges—nor was he interested in reporting or news gathering. And still he himself could not understand his irresistible desire to be present in the court for this particular case. Every time there was a hearing, he would bunk college and class, reach well on time, all alone, without his college friends, and keep staring fixedly at Daataa Anand.

His total absorption in the case was beginning to annoy his girlfriend Seema, a lovely, mature young girl. She grumbled, 'What is this, Kishen! Are you taking this case up as a subject for your PhD.?' The other day she had been waiting for Kishen to meet her as he had promised, after her college got over. The very impressive grey building of the Patna Womens' College is right across the High Court. Kishen Das had to just cross the road and be there, but he had not come. Everybody had left. She alone stood, waiting at the gates of her college. For the boys in and around Patna, the gates of the Patna Women's College were the portals of heaven. And as ardent devotees, any number of boys would gather outside the college, paying homage to the beauties within. Seema felt very odd standing there alone with all those boys and men passing by, looking at her and trying to draw her attention. That day the trial arguments kept stretching and Kishen got so involved he forgot his promise to Seema. This was the first time that Kishen had not kept his word. Seema was very hurt, upset, angry and actually quite bewildered with Kishen's behaviour.

The next time Kishen and Seema met, she did not care to control her annoyance. She showered Kishen with sarcasm. 'Oh! So you've finally got time for us lesser mortals! The court proceedings, it seems, can do without the judge or the pleaders, but not without you, is it?' Her fair complexion turned red with anger.

'Sorry, Seema, no it's not like . . .'

'What? There is no need to be sorry. After all, you seem

to be Daataa Anand's most faithful devotee, ardent admirer, trustworthy friend and . . .'

Before Seema completed her sentence, Kishen lost his temper. For a second, Seema was frightened that he might even become violent. Shaking in anger, Kishen hissed, emphasizing every word, 'DON'T. YOU. EVER. CALL. ME. DAATAA. ANAND'S. DEVOTEE. AND. FRIEND! You can abuse me, call me names, say anything you like. I will accept . . . tolerate . . . but Daataa's admirer, *I will never be!* Trembling with anger, he pushed her away.

Seema was stunned. This wasn't the Kishen she knew. She had always appreciated his cool temperament. She had never seen him so ruffled. What had Daataa Anand done to him? Why was he reacting so insanely?

After a while, as Kishen came to his senses, he realized how angry he'd been and how wrongly he had reacted. How could he have behaved like this with Seema? He apologized profusely, over and over again.

Seema, still unsure of what had happened, made up her mind. She would never bring up this topic again with Kishen. If he found the case so interesting, so be it. After all, he was a responsible citizen of this country, and it was his duty to keep an eye on the growing criminal tendencies of society. She loved Kishen too much to fight over trivial issues. She decided to invest in the virtue of patience.

Files and papers pertaining to the case were strewn all over the table of the judges in the courtroom. While the lawyers were still busy advocating their points, Justice Shankar looked at his files, turning the pages and jotting down some points. He suddenly came across some sketches on a white sheet.

The first picture was of Justice Shankar's car, with the number plate clearly drawn. In the next, the car had been blown to pieces, and the severed head of Justice Shankar, drawn with red ink, was flying up in the sky.

For a second the judge was numb, not because of the drawing, but with astonishment at the impudence of the person who would have put the drawings in his file! He was very sure that whoever it was would definitely be sitting in the courtroom at that time to see his reaction. So in a nonchalant response, he picked up the drawing, lifted it a little above the table, and tore it into pieces. He wanted to show those people that he was not intimidated by their threats. They could not harm him, and they should accept the fact that they could not do to him what they had done to the three previous judges. He was too strong, too seasoned and too experienced for them to crack.

The two people, sitting on the side benches in the courtroom, waiting eagerly to see Justice Shankar's reaction, were thoroughly disappointed. They had expected the judge to collapse, shivering with fear and perhaps suffer an immediate heart attack like the earlier judge. They had hoped that like previous times, the case would be put on hold till a new bench was formed. They were depending heavily on delaying tactics because they knew that this was a tough case. It was almost impossible to save Daataa Anand. He was out on bail, and until his guilt was established, he could lead a normal life. So all they had to do was to manage to extend the case as far as possible. In fact, his devotees were practically sure that it would not be possible to save their esteemed guru. He had been caught at the wrong time at the wrong place, and no one could make things right for him.

Now they also understood that Justice Shankar was not an ordinary person. They would not be able to influence him or his judgement with these bullying tactics. It was a hopeless situation, but they were not ready to give up yet. Extraordinary adversaries demand extraordinary strategies. They would have to try and devise something unusual the next time. And try they would, right till the end.

6

The Advocate Association's canteen was, as usual, full of noises and people. Here, lawyers exchanged notes over a cup of tea with tasty samosas and syrupy gulab jamuns. Some of the more miserly lawyers took their clients along to foot the bill—even when the bill amounted to less than two digits. The conversation, as expected, was Justice Shankar's court.

The two people who had planted the pictures in Justice Shankar's files arrived in the canteen, looking grim. They were disappointed by Justice Shankar's reaction to their trap. They stood at the canteen doors for a moment, but since they did not like people appreciating and favouring the judge, they went outside.

The High Court was situated in an impressive compound. The gardens were meticulously laid out and well-maintained. Flowering red, yellow and orange cannas adorning the green lawns lent colour and brightness. The general atmosphere was such that it would lift the moods of anyone who stepped into the court premises. But the two walked past the fresh, fragrant lawns morosely, without even glancing at the bed of beautiful roses in full bloom, flirting with the gentle breeze. They walked straight to the gates where many cycle rickshaws stood, their hoods folded down. They were the most convenient, cheap and environment-friendly vehicles for moving around in Patna. One could see any number of rickshaws occupied by lawyers in black coats and the white neckband, plying in all directions.

One of the two dejected men wanted to hire a rickshaw, but the other one signalled 'no'. He did not want the rickshaw puller listening to their conversation and so they decided to walk back to their homes.

In those days, Patna was the ideal city to live in. It had ample open spaces and plenty of greenery, especially around the High Court. But who cared for nature's bounties when circumstances were not favourable! Definitely not Daataa's two crestfallen soldiers. They looked at each other once they hit Baily Road outside the High Court gates. One of them whispered, 'What a creature! Nothing affects him.'

The other one agreed. 'Perhaps he thinks that our threats are for fun. We must show him some real action now. Make him understand that we mean business!'

'Yes. But now at least we have access to his house through that guard. How neatly he inserted that drawing amongst papers kept in the car, and that idiot driver could not even make out why he had opened the door.'

'No, the guard was smart enough to tell the driver that it was just a routine security check.'

They laughed, reflecting delightedly on their first victory.

'Another good thing is that the guard is armed. If this damn judge does not behave and listen to our straight talk, then we will have to make a much bigger noise to get the point across to him. He keeps asking unnecessary questions in the court. Such a bully he is, and did you notice, he was even prodding the lawyer and asking embarrassing, leading questions. He thought he would get to the bottom of the case in just one sitting. He is crazy.' They released their frustration by abusing the judge and the advocates.

'Exactly, and did you hear him say, "Why are the eyewitnesses disappearing? They gave statements earlier without fear—what or who stops them from coming forward now?" I felt like saying, you and your arrogant, treacherous questions, my lord!'

'But what is wrong with our government pleader? I thought he was well tutored and yet like an idiot he blurted, "We've tried our best, my lord! But they are becoming wiser it seems!"'

'And that horrible monster of a judge, immediately caught on the word "wiser" saying, "What do you mean by wiser? Are they benefiting in any way by staying away?" Thank god our lawyer shut him up. He is smart enough not to miss a chance to interrupt and say, "What he means, my lord, is that they have now become wise enough to understand the word perjury, they realize that they cannot lie under oath."'

'Luckily, that sloppy, idiotic government pleader got the hint and kept quiet after that.'

'If that stupid public prosecutor cares for his life then he better do his homework, learn his lessons and lose the case for our benefit,' replied the other.

'Yes, but we need to tame this wild boar, too—the judge. Tell the guard to keep an eye on his son and inform us on who all are his friends. Which places does he go to? What time does he leave home and when does he return etc.? And if possible, ask him also to point the gun at the son to frighten him and the family.'

'You know what! I think it will be a good idea to blast a bomb at his gate one day!' said the other, getting really excited. 'He better understand that we are serious about the content of those letters, otherwise one day we will do to him exactly what he did to our letter in the court.'

They both smiled.

'Did the newspaper chap do his bit?'

'He said he will do it tomorrow.'

'Good, keep the pressure on from all possible corners. Make life so miserable for the judge that he has no option but to run away from here.'

What the duo did not know was that Kishen Das was following them close behind. The moment Kishen had heard them talking about the judge, he'd became alert. He'd quickly overtaken the two and then concentrated hard in order to listen to them.

Unfortunately, the two strangers started talking in whispers. Kishen was not very sure of what they were saying, but they were definitely planning something ghastly. Once in a while he heard the words 'judge', 'bomb', 'guard' and so on. He inferred that these people were planning to harm Justice Shankar and his family. Kishen got very worried and concerned for the judge's safety, thinking that nothing must happen to him.

Justice Shankar, he had realized over time as he closely followed the case, was just the right man to handle this case—strong, brave, conscientious, just, honest and truthful. And these were the sterling qualities which seemed to be irking these unsavoury characters. The bloody swines!

Kishen was so angry he felt like beating these men up to a bloody pulp. But he quickly controlled his emotions. It was infinitely better for him to exercise caution in this matter. Any precipitate action on his part could potentially boomerang and hurt Justice Shankar. Kishen quietly kept walking and listening to their conversation.

Daataa Anand had an extensive organization and just as these two people were given the charge of handling and, if required, eliminating Justice Shankar and his family, others were given the task of 'managing' the SP, the eyewitnesses, and the advocates pleading on behalf of the government.

But before anything else, the doctor attending on Daataa when he was still in jail was one of the first ones to be tackled. The poor doctor got so frightened that every night he changed his bedroom, from one room to the other, bolting and locking up the windows and the doors, then checking and rechecking to see if the locks were firmly secured. Still not feeling safe enough, he would move from his house to his friend's or relatives' homes, and yet, keep awake and restless the whole night, eyes and ears wide open to pick up unfamiliar faces and footsteps of people coming to kill him—the way they had done the first time they asked him to give medical advice for Daataa's release from jail, and he had refused. His mental condition had become like that of a tiny mouse, hiding away not only from a cat but from the entire world. Only after he managed to secure bail for Daataa on medical grounds was he left alone.

Doing all this was easy for Daataa's men. They did not have to work hard on it. In this poor country, money work like magic. A wad of notes is any day more powerful than a sword, gun or tanks. Anyone can be bought over, killed or managed with this powerful weapon.

7

Daataa Anand began his day with yoga and meditation. After that he would dance to the bhajan, 'Anandam hi Anandam . . .' along with his disciples. Next on the routine was a discourse followed by a few more bhajans. Daataa had a number of foreigners as disciples. They were given a privileged status and sat right in front. Daataa made sure that they were comfortable, and every morning he would enquire about their well-being.

Daataa's discourses were very impressive. He talked about the very basic things of life, giving practical examples. He explained human emotions and feelings in such a way that it touched a chord in everybody's heart. Each person listening to the discourse felt that it was him or her who was being addressed. Daataa provided simple solutions to complex problems. People felt relieved, relaxed and happy just by listening to him.

Daataa recognized all his followers by their first names. He did not just share their pain and problems, but also showed them the path to nirvana. Such was his charisma that to his disciples, it seemed as if Daataa had taken all their burdens upon himself to make them happy. Who would not like to be a part of such an organization? People simply handed over their woes to their guru and danced, day and night, to 'Anandam hi anandam . . .' And the number of followers only kept increasing.

Nobody knew anything about Daataa's family history. It was almost as if the man had been born adult, a full-fledged guru—it is impossible to check the antecedents of such a man. In any case, many gurus have been known to have sacrificed their homes and their families in pursuit of truth and spirituality. This fact further strengthened the reticence about asking uncomfortable questions.

But yes, people had a vague idea that he had spent his childhood somewhere in Hazaribagh, Bihar. What had it been like? Who had influenced him to take this path while he was growing up? It seemed that these queries could be answered only by Rachna—the woman who claimed to be his wife and was now untraceable.

Rachna knew that Daataa had no knowledge of his father. His mother had told everybody that his father had died two weeks before Daataa was born. The father was an orphan and had no relatives she knew of. When Daataa was born, his mother had no option but to wrap the child in a torn sari and carry him all the way from Calcutta to Hazaribagh. At that time she had named him Anurag Chowdhury.

Travelling by train and without a ticket, she'd managed to reach her distant grand-aunt's house in Hazaribagh. Nani was very old and incapacitated and she had no one to take care of her except a battery of servants. Her children lived abroad. She was rich and for her, this sudden arrival of a relative was a boon. She was only too happy to not ask her grand-niece, Daataa's mother, uncomfortable questions. Her prayers had been answered, she had found company and a bundle of joy in her grand-niece's arms. And Daataa's mother blessed her stars; she could not have asked for a better heaven.

But the neighbours were not as generous. They had to satisfy their curiosity. After all, it concerned their neighbourhood. They had to know everyone and everything that was happening next door. They bombarded the ageing, rich woman with many questions—'Who is this woman? If she is a relative, then where was she all this while? Why has she come alone? Who is the father of the child? Where is he? Why did she not go to her in-laws?' Anurag's mother became the target of nasty brickbats and malicious gossip.

However, Anurag's mother was made of stern stuff. Having a shrewd idea that she would face uncomfortable questions, she had come prepared. She had made friends with a nurse in the hospital where she had given birth to Daataa. From the nurse, she had received the information that a thirty-five year-old man lay dead in the mortuary. He had died in a road accident just two weeks before Anurag was born. His face was badly smashed and no one had come forward to claim his body. The man had a piece of paper in his pocket which had just the name Chowdhury written on it—and, therefore, the dead body was called Chowdhury.

Anurag's mother used this information well. She claimed the dead man to be her husband, her child's father, and lamented her fate that she had been widowed too soon. Her life became easier after that.

To further bolster the myth, Anurag's mother would start weeping so profusely at the mention of her husband that people stopped probing. 'Poor widow . . . it's a tough life . . .' they'd say at the end of all their queries.

When Anurag was very small, he wanted to know all about his father and kept pestering his mother to tell him stories about him. He remembered how his mother had slapped him once and then broken down, crying and hugging the stunned child. When he grew up, he made sure that he did not bring up questions about his father ever again because he could not see tears in his mother's eyes. He cared a lot for his mother and would never go against her wishes. At the same time, all his life, Anurag was subtly made to understand that his mother had had a very tough life, looking after Nani and bringing him up all by herself.

Much later, Anurag fell in love with Rachna, a prostitute. In an emotionally weak moment, he told her about the suspicion he had always had about his mother. He had a niggling doubt that his mother had also been a prostitute. Anurag had come to this conclusion from the way his mother became fidgety and nervous at the mere mention of Calcutta. He also found it extremely strange that his mother never talked about her past under any circumstances. These were flimsy reasons, but there was no way he could find out for sure, so Anurag only speculated.

However, when Rachna entered Anurag's life, he felt relieved that his mother would perhaps understand his choice. But he was wrong. His mother was furious at their desire to get married. He tried hard to convince his mother, but she was unrelenting. When he persisted, his mother used her trump card—her tears. She made it very clear that a prostitute could never become his wife. Her final instructions were, 'She will ruin your life. Break off all links with her before she does this to you. I will never accept Rachna, and that's final!' Chapter closed. No debate was welcome on the subject.

Anurag then vowed that he would marry only Rachna or stay single all his life. He knew that his mother would be hurt to hear this. So without any further discussions on the matter, he left for Calcutta under the pretext of going for higher studies.

In Calcutta, he spent his weekends with Rachna in one of those dilapidated, congested Beliagachi rooms that were so small barely one cot could fit in with difficulty. This suffocating accommodation was dimly lit, had a cot with stained sheet, and reeked of stale country liquor, cheap perfume and dried up gajras.

But for Anurag, when he rested his head on Rachna's

lap, he was in heaven. He found solace in her company and talked to her in detail about his future plans, his big dreams. He asked Rachna to marry him then and there but Rachna knew that it was not possible. Anurag was still in college and had no source of income. It was with great difficulty that he was meeting his college expenses, and whatever little he got from home, he spent on Rachna.

He would read books on Swami Vivekanand and was profoundly influenced by his philosophy. He used to tell Rachna how Swami Vivekanand had travelled extensively in India. How he used to take care of the poor, the downtrodden, the sick and the elderly. How he took it upon himself to wipe their tears and miseries. How he was concerned about the progress of his country. How he worried about the falling moral standards of his countrymen and how Western influence on our culture troubled him. And it pained him to see how rapidly the status of women was deteriorating in Indian society. He wanted the world to know about the rich cultural heritage and traditions of this great country.

Suddenly, Anurag's eyes lit up. He had found a solution to all his problems. His dreams seemed within reach now. He had found his goal. He had decided upon the future course of action—he would follow Vivekanand's ideologies and preach his philosophy to the ignorant world (with some inputs of his own too), and reinforce the supremacy of India over other countries in this field.

One day, Rachna heard an interesting story about Vivekanand and narrated it to Anurag. She told him how

Swami Vivekanand would travel far and wide in search of knowledge—sometimes in disguise, because by then he had become famous and people had started recognizing him. On one such sojourn, he came to the court of a king. Music and dance was in full swing, and the audience was listening to one particular court singer.

What would a saint do in such mehfils? I must stay away from all kinds of temptation, the swami thought to himself. Even watching a seductive woman perform is like a sin—he must stay away. He got up to go.

The singer had recognized him, as the glow on his face was difficult to hide behind his disguise. She addressed him and started singing a bhajan: 'Sumdarshee hai naam tihaaro, chahe to paap haro, awaguna chit na dharo, prabhu ji . . .'

This bhajan challenged the pious man! It said, 'You are known for treating your subjects equally, you can simply overlook my vices, show your greatness by pardoning me and treat me like you treat others.'

Vivekanand understood her plea and realized that she was a normal human being too, capable of committing mistakes like anyone else. Then why should she be looked down upon, her profession ridiculed? The devotional song shook him up completely and touched a chord deep in his heart. The saint thanked the woman for teaching him a great lesson.

Anurag was much influenced by this story. He saw a reflection of his own self in this. He felt his own greatness was no less compared to Swami Vivekanand's. After all, wasn't he, too, providing the same service to humankind?

Giving support and preparing to marry a fallen woman who had been shunned by society? A thought flashed in his mind: could he possibly be a reincarnation of Swami Vivekanand?

He got hold of the lyrics of that bhajan and read the lines a number of times, trying to understand the meaning of the lines and the depth of thought behind it. But the more he tried to understand, the more the meaning slipped out of his grasp. Ultimately, he came to the conclusion that life is too vast and too complicated to understand and explain in its entirety. It cannot be defined, and is different for different individuals.

But he was very sure of one thing—no matter how comfortable or happy one may look, everyone in this world is unhappy. The smallest of problems take up giant proportions when it concerns one, but seem petty when others face them.

Thus, Anurag made up his mind. He would fill the gap left behind by Swami Vivekanand. He would help people understand life, find eternal bliss and happiness. He would show them the path of spirituality and happiness, help them attain nirvana and make them happy. Sadly, even in what he thought was his enlightened state, Anurag failed to realize that he was neither Swami Vivekanand nor anywhere remotely close to him.

Vivekanand was truth personified, his love for god and fellow human beings sprang from the depth of his heart; he had researched, studied, meditated and sacrificed. He had tested his own purity, strength, weaknesses and limitations, taken tough decisions and had understood his own self completely before starting to preach or voice his thoughts.

On the other hand stood Anurag, a man who aspired to be a spiritual guide to his fellow beings, but an individual with little connection to his inner self. How could a person who could not rise above the limitations of his own ego teach to others the way to attain everlasting peace? On which progressive path would he lead his followers?

However, since the idea was now firmly entrenched in his mind, Anurag wore special saffron-coloured robes, just like Vivekanand, and embarked on his mission. Rachna was his first disciple, and he started by explaining his tenets of life to her: this life is very short, don't let it go waste. The past is over and the future is not in our hands. Your present is the only time that belongs to you, so live your present with zest. In any case, you live just once. Why not forget your miseries and pains, accept your fellow beings with open arms and an open heart, live life fully. Sing and dance with fervour in appreciation and praise of the lord almighty. Think of your own soul, make it happy, and forget what the world says. Don't worry about the world—whether they like you or not is immaterial, be happy with yourself, be bold and enjoy every moment to the hilt. 'Be happy and make happy'—because that is how god wants to see you.

Anurag was so thrilled with his creative self and the thoughts that took the shape of a new religious sect that he danced all night holding Rachna in his arms, kissing her all over.

He was euphoric. He was the conqueror. The earth lay at his feet while he danced in the skies, swinging between stars and colouring the rainbows—and it was he who would teach humanity the true meaning of life and love, joy and sorrow, pain and penitence. Through him would mankind discover the significance of their own lives. And thus was 'Daataa Anand' born.

8

Justice Shankar was an early riser. He delighted in the serenity of his garden every morning and enjoyed sharing the first rays of dawn with his plants. He walked along, admiring the fresh blooms swaying softly in the gentle breeze and felt truly one with nature.

Meanwhile, Meera would make tea and bring the tray to the veranda. It would take a little while for the tea to brew, so she would join her husband in appreciating the riotous display of colours, the variety of the new flowers and the cosily wrapped buds waiting their turn to bloom.

This had been their routine since ages. Their children would join them one by one, eyes barely open, but not wanting to miss out on the pleasure of participating in their parents' light bantering and a collective, humorous start to the day. Judge Saab was known for his jovial moods and he was at his best during mornings. This is how the family began every day, in a very positive way.

But today things were different. Justice Shankar sat quietly brooding. The previous day's episode in court was still troubling him. Who could have put that paper with the threats to his life in his file?

'Are you all right?' Meera asked.

'Yes, I am all right, but something has been bothering me since yesterday,' he said.

Meera probed. 'Yes, I can see that you are disturbed. What is it?'

'One of our trustworthy servants—the peon, the driver or the gardener—has some problem with us . . .'

Meera asked, 'Why? What happened?'

Still deep in thought, Judge Saab said, 'I don't know, but somebody has surely been hurt by our actions. We should ask each servant. And if anyone has any problem at all, we must try to solve it,' he said, looking up.

'Ask them for one problem and they will tell you about the hundreds they must have, money being the major one. How will you help them? How much can you give to so many of them? As it is, even we face problems . . .' Meera's voice trailed away.

Justice Shankar responded, 'Still, we will have to talk to them. And I don't think money is their major problem—they are used to doing without it. No, it is not money. They know they can always ask us for loans, and so far we have been able to help them every time they've asked. No, it is something much deeper than that. For some reason, someone's feelings have been bruised, and you know, Meera, how painful it can be when you are hurt. You feel dejected, you lose faith, you lose hope, you get angry. This should not happen to them. They should not lose their hope, faith and trust in us.'

Meera, who was listening intently, asked, 'But what has happened? Has anyone said anything?'

Justice Shankar did not give her an answer. He did not want her to worry about the paper in his file. He just looked the other way.

Meera persisted, 'What do you want to do? Should I call them here?'

Shankar replied, 'No. I have not been to see them recently. I must go to their rooms and ask after them.'

Meera knew that Judge Saab usually did not say these things, but she also knew that when he did, he meant every word of it. And so she simply kept quiet. She realized how much their servants meant to him. He cared for them so much that the moment somebody even sneezed, Judge Saab would start preparing homeopathic medicine for him. Actually, that was the judge's retirement plan: to treat the poor free of cost, with care, compassion and homeopathic medicine. Meera recollected how he had given a supportive shoulder to their old servant Birju when he had had an acute bronchial attack. The judge had personally rushed him to the hospital and sat with Birju till he was out of danger. Then he had also taken care of the complete expenses of all the barat meals at his driver's daughter's wedding. The servants, too, had deep affection and respect for the judge.

Before being appointed a judge of the Patna High Court, Justice Shankar was the member of a tribunal. It was a transferable job and whenever he was transferred, all his secretaries, assistants, typists, clerks, peons, everyone he had come into contact with, used to cry like small children. Meera would often hear them say as they were leaving, 'Sir, you have been like god to us. You are the first officer who gave us so much respect, shared our happiness and sorrows alike, helped us whenever we needed, without our asking for it. Sir, we will become orphans again, please don't go, sir, we need you here.' The same scene repeated itself when they left Calcutta, Madras, Bombay, the cities the judge was posted to before Patna.

His humility, kindness and the very strong bonds of friendship that he established with his fellow workers, together with his compassionate nature, won everyone over. People were ready to lay down their lives for him. Had they known of the present threat to him and his family, they all would have come and guarded him twenty-four hours, risking their own lives without a second thought. But here, for some unknown reasons, things were different. Justice Shankar felt let down by the very people he trusted the most. His own staff! What had gone wrong? No outsider could get access to this file—it had to be the work of some insider. Who had joined hands with the criminals and for what? He hated himself for suspecting his staff. They were too dear to him. But this was a serious matter, and he knew he had to talk to each one of them personally and see if he could help them. He was engrossed in his thoughts when the ringing of a cycle

bell attracted his attention. It was the newspaper vendor. A
narrow road encircled the house and the man used to cycle
around to the triangular veranda at the back of the house
and hand over the newspaper there.

In those days, Patna used to publish just two newspapers,
the *Indian Nation* and the *Searchlight*. Along with these two
newspapers, the vendor also left one magazine on the table
and turned back in a hurry. Meera saw the magazine and
called him back. She told him that they did not wish to buy
the magazine. He turned around, stood his cycle on its stand
and came to the veranda, but refused to take the magazine
back. He tried to convince the judge, 'Sir, please keep this
magazine. It is very good and sells a lot!'

Judge Saab politely refused and said that they did not
want it.

'Sir, listen to me, please take this, otherwise, sir, you don't
know, but you will get into trouble.'

Judge Saab smiled at him and said, 'Thank you for your
concern, but no, we don't want the magazine.'

'Sir, you don't know. You are inviting trouble.'

By now Justice Shankar was getting annoyed. 'Why are
you insisting?'

'Because we have been asked to,' was the response.

'Who has asked you?'

The newspaper guy suddenly came very close to Justice
Shankar. Meera panicked. What was all this about? She
called out to Birju, their faithful servant.

The newspaper vendor was a thin, wiry man with keen
eyes. He bent towards the judge and whispered, 'Sir, you don't

know, the prime minister has asked us to report to her if any government servant refuses to buy this. Sir, this magazine is *Surya*, edited by the PM's daughter-in-law. Listen to me, sir, don't defy orders, believe me, otherwise you will repent it.'

Justice Shankar was getting sick of this. He picked up the magazine, stuffed it in the vendor's hands, and said very coolly, 'Please go and tell your prime minister or whoever she is that I have refused to take it. And I don't give a damn about the consequences!'

'Sir, just for a few rupees you are picking up fight with her. Don't do it, sir, you don't know the danger.' He tried to sell it again.

Justice Shankar was losing his patience by now, 'Look, if you want money, take double the price of this magazine from me, but I will not keep *Surya*. Some Emergency this is! You need permission to sit down and stand up! Huh!'

By now Birju had reached the veranda and he sent the newspaper chap out from there.

About two kilometres away from the judge's house, two men were standing, waiting for the vendor. They were the ones who had given the vendor twenty rupees to deliver the magazine to Justice Shankar's house. The miscreants were only too happy to know that they had managed to rub Justice Shankar the wrong way. Their game plan was simple: take away the judge's peace of mind; get him so fed up and angry that he would react unduly to the Emergency and invite the wrath of the supreme command and thus get transferred or better still, dismissed.

9

The number of thieves, dacoits, killers, cheats and frauds was escalating every day. Times were such that the concept of right and wrong had taken a complete somersault. The supreme leader was idolized by a number of opportunists who were ready to do anything in her name and get handsome rewards in return. They used the political Emergency to take personal revenge on their enemies. The situation was such that people would murder at the slightest provocation, people disappeared overnight, and there was a general breakdown of law and order.

The general public was frightened. People did not have the courage to speak up against the wrongs of the government. They feared talking to each other in trains, buses or any public place. It was impossible to find the perpetrators of crime. Who were they? They wondered if it was the government taking those ruthless measures against its innocent, unsuspecting subjects? Or was it that personal vendettas were being settled by the official machinery? The infamous midnight knock on anyone's door had become a nightmare for the citizen. As it was, the press was muzzled and no one had any idea about the extent to which the authorities were misusing their power. Who was right and who was wrong?

People became suspicious of each other. They were scared of informers even amongst their closest friends. People were hushed to silence by their well-wishers the moment they opened their mouths to condemn the rampant corruption and high-handedness of the government. They were told, for instance, about people like the train traveller who was arrested and deboarded from the train because he had the audacity to find faults with the Emergency and the supreme command. The rule of law had ceased to exist.

The forced silence was deafening, anger was boiling inside every citizen's heart; they hated being marginalized and wanted to scream, shout, abuse and call names, but the Emergency diktats forbade them from opposing any order. Such was the state of affairs.

Telephones were being tapped. Fundamental rights were suspended. The country had lost its voice. Democracy was in a coma, and it was allowed to breathe only through the governmental machinery. There was an overdose of oppression. States were reeling under the baton of dictatorship.

In the throes of a slow, asphyxiated death, the nation needed oxygen. However, no one dared to break open the

windows to let in some fresh air. Justice Shankar dared to
do just that. He challenged the establishment with his small
but very bold judgement against the government, inviting its
wrath. His judgement was in favour of the rebels tutored by
the leader Jaiprakash Narain and it condemned the atrocities
of the government.

Daataa's disciples were thrilled! They felt that the judge
was digging his own grave with such judgements. Good for
him and for us, they said. Let the government take him to
task, it only makes our job that much easier. Now that he is
cornered, the only possible fate for Justice Shankar is defeat
and destruction. If the government does not punish him, we
will, was their promise to Daataa.

And then, the supreme leader decided to visit Patna. All
the judges, including the chief justice, were sent invitations
to receive her at the Patna airport. They were asked to bring
the invitation card along for security purposes. The card
sounded more like an order than a request. Never before had
any High Court judge been given such orders. For the first
time in the history of free India, civil servants were being
made to feel like lackeys who must unquestioningly obey
orders and be at the beck and call of a higher power.

Justice Shankar looked at his card disgustedly and threw
it in the dustbin. He wondered what it was that the high
command was trying to prove. That the country's leader was
more than a prime minister? That she was queen, empress,
tyrant rolled into one?

He found this invitation very insulting to the judiciary.
He decided he would not go. The leader could do whatever

she wished, but the judge felt such arrogance did not befit a prime minister of a democracy and, therefore, it could not be tolerated.

The other judges who attended the welcoming ceremony at the airport returned fuming and fretting with anger. There were no sitting arrangements for them; to them it seemed that just because she'd lost her case with the Allahabad High Court, Madam Gandhi wanted to humiliate and take revenge on the rest of the judiciary. It was a petty gesture and a real shame. And the humiliation didn't stop there. Every judge's attendance was checked at the airport. Every card had a number written in one corner, which was torn and kept aside at the entrance. Justice Shankar was marked absent. He was not bothered but his brother judges were concerned about him. They tried to tell him that perhaps it wasn't wise to show so much courage. Prudence was definitely a virtue in the times they lived in. But Justice Shankar simply did not care. He believed that he was treading the path of truth and justice very sincerely. It was their leader who had lost her sincerity of purpose.

The press was not supposed to quote or publish Justice Shankar's anti-establishment assertions. It could influence the general public and that would be disastrous. Even otherwise, Patna had a bad name. It was here that Jaiprakash Narain had started a movement against the Emergency, and the students had joined in full force with large numbers. As a result, Mrs Gandhi and her followers were a bit over-concerned about this state.

Underneath his anger and irritation, Judge Saab felt a

deep pity for people like their leader. They could not see their true reflection in the mirror. Convinced about their invincibility, such people would fail to see the sly smiles and winks behind their backs.

In a small town like Patna, wagging tongues play a bigger and better role than any newspaper. And irrespective of stories being printed, or not, in the local dailies, people learnt of Justice Shankar's daring statements and defiance in no time. In fact, newspapers were not really required.

At the Fraser Road dak bungalow crossing stood a paan shop, gaily decorated with mirrors and magazine cut-outs of popular cine stars. This was the hub for all juicy gossip and the most active and authentic source of local information— especially as a counter-force to the restricting commands of the Emergency.

'You know, buddy, lots of people have been saying that Judge Saab has been cheeky again and has refused to receive Madam at the airport.' Such stories about the judge going against the government and snubbing the supreme leader herself gave Daataa's camp a lot of happiness and satisfaction. They dreamt about the dismissal of the judge within a day or two and would start dancing with more gusto and jubilation.

But when nothing happened even after a week, they started wondering about Madam. Didn't she have any self-respect? How could she tolerate this insult and not take any action! They started planning their next move afresh.

The two men assigned to destabilize the judge had no idea that Kishen Das had begun following them like a shadow.

Sometimes he would change his appearance so that they wouldn't recognize him and doubt his intentions. The more he heard them use foul language and plan to eliminate Justice Shankar, the more he would seethe. Sometimes he had problems keeping calm but he had no option. He wondered how anybody could kill innocent people in order to save one merciless killer?

Sometimes he felt like going straight to the police and informing them about the danger to Justice Shankar and his family's life. But he could imagine their reaction very well. They would probably say something like, 'Police has armed guards posted for Justice Shankar's safety at his residence. Nothing will happen to him. Tell us if you know of some concrete plans that they are going to execute.' No, definitely no point going to the police—it would not help.

Unscathed, unfazed and ignorant about all the planning and plotting going on behind his back, Justice Shankar, with all his dignity and his pure, pious thoughts, would sit in meditation and pray devotedly with all his heart and mind. He would talk at length with Meera about the failing moral standards of the government and the growing corruption amongst the young officers. All of it was demoralizing for the future of this country and its society.

Justice Shankar's elder daughter Rajani had come from Calcutta for a few days. He enjoyed discussing all kinds of issues with her, and he had become best friend to her little son, playing and talking with him as if he, too, were a child. The judge's strength was his courageous and fearless mind which his opponents were bent upon breaking. Every day they would challenge him with some new threat, obstacle and tension, trying to make life difficult for him. So far, he had managed to surmount all obstacles, but how long would he be able to walk barefoot on shattered glass?

10

Kishen Das wanted to talk to his father about the court case against Daataa Anand. He wanted to tell him how some people were after Justice Shankar's life. But he knew that his father was not interested. The first time that Kishen had broached the topic, his father had told him to shut up and lay off the case as it was in no way connected to him. 'Have you gone mad? What do you have to do with the court and its cases?' his father had furiously said. 'Don't waste your time on these useless things. Just concentrate on your studies. You think the civil service examination is a joke? I studied day and night for months together and only then could I get through in the third attempt. And just see the outcome, how comfortable we are now, this big house, servants' quarters, free telephone, free peons and the many other perks. We have so much respect in society! People want to make friends with us, know us. Do you know why? Because I am an IAS officer. Come over to my office one day and I will show you how much power I wield!'

Mr Das, as usual, was blowing his own trumpet. He never failed to emphasize the fact that he was a member of the privileged Indian Administrative Services (IAS) profession. Kishen Das had heard this lecture umpteen times and it was now deeply and firmly imprinted in his memory. He could repeat verbatim what his father was saying. Also, by now, Kishen was immune to his father's haranguings. He coolly replied, 'I don't want to become an IAS officer like you. I just can't bear to salute the useless, corrupt, uneducated, pot-bellied, uncouth chief minister and his gang. Thank you very much.'

This ignited his father's ire. 'Then what will you do? With economics honours as your subject, you cannot become an engineer or a doctor! Being a clerk or a peon is your only option, unless you want to become a labourer or cut grass for others!'

In those days, a student could think of only these three careers—the civil services, followed by medicine or engineering. And if you were not in one of these professions, then you were useless, a nobody.

Kishen Das was not hassled and promptly told his father that he would work with some private firm.

His father was now incensed with his ignorance and disgustedly said, 'Oh, I see! Yes indeed. Private firm. You want to go door to door selling oil and soap! Have you ever thought about my position and dignity in society? All the big bosses from Tata and Bata keep standing at my door from

morning till evening—only then are they able to see me, and
you want to work under them? What a splendid thought!
Private firm, eh! God put some sense into the puny brains
of this stupid son of mine. Disgraceful! Shameful!'

Kishen Das's father held an important post in the Bihar
government. He knew about the ongoing case of Daataa
Anand in Justice Shankar's court. He also knew Justice
Shankar's views on Madam Gandhi and the Emergency.
He was quite sure that sooner or later, Justice Shankar
would have to give up his arrogance and toe the line like
the rest of the other government officers. And until he did
that, Kishen's father wanted to stay away from the judge.
But this dim-witted son of his did not know what he was
doing—so enamoured was he of Justice Shankar that he
idolized him and thought no end of him and was forever
singing his praises.

Mr Das had severe objections to what he thought was a
totally senseless fancy of the boy. He wanted him to realize
that all this could put his father into trouble. Anybody could
report to the high command about his son's allegiance to
Justice Shankar and Mr Das would have to come up with
convincing explanations. And if he failed to make excuses,
he could get blacklisted and shunted to some obscure posting
in a corner of the state! And so he never encouraged Kishen
to talk about Daataa's case.

Kishen had lost his mother when he was just twelve years
old and his father doted on him. Mr Das was forever worried
and anxious about his son's well-being. But they had a very
strange relationship. They took pleasure in holding absolutely

opposing views on every issue. The moment they came face to face with each other, furious debates and discussions would start and soon turn into verbal battles. They would always start talking in normal tones, but in no time the pitch and volume both escalated. Kishen loved to tease his father and sometimes, just to annoy him, he would do crazy things.

One day, Mr Das brought samosas especially for his son. He loved to see Kishen's face light up at the sight of samosas. He kept waiting for a long time, but Kishen was nowhere to be found. When he rang up Seema—Mr Das knew about her—she told him that Kishen had not come to see her though she had waited for him for a long time. Perhaps he was still in Justice Shankar's court.

Mr Das's face reddened with rage on hearing that. This indisciplined son of his must simply be taught a lesson! How could he be so irresponsible? His temper soaring every passing second, he began pacing the portico.

Kishen saw his father from a distance. He knew that his father marched up and down like this only when he was in a fit of rage. He immediately took a detour into a back lane, quietly parked his bike in a neighbour's compound and tip-toed into his house after jumping over the back wall with practised precision. He went straight to his room, flung himself on the cot, and covered himself from head to toe with a sheet. Then he called the servant and asked him to inform his father that he had fever and so was sleeping.

On hearing about his son's fever Mr Das forgot his anger and the vow to teach him a lesson. Extremely worried and concerned, he ran to his bedside. Kishen's eyes were closed.

Mr Das gently touched his forehead. There was no fever. He understood that Kishen was trying to fool him. Holding the mattress on one side, he jerked it up and Kishen fell down on the ground. He quickly stood up and took the offence-is-the-best-defence stance. 'What is this, Pop? My bones could have broken! Do you know why I get those horrible fits? You are the reason. Is this the way to treat your son? You are no less than Hitler, do you know that? You are the one I am scared of even in my dreams. How can the doctor help me? He needs to see you to understand my problem first . . .'

Suddenly, Kishen observed that his father had turned very quiet. He looked into his eyes and saw tears. Kishen was ashamed of himself—how mean it was of him to say those harsh words and hurt his father! He felt very small. His father cared so much for him and this was what he gave him in return. He repented every word of what he had just said, and felt like crying. Kishen then hugged his father tight and apologized profusely. His father looked stern, and was a strict disciplinarian, but Kishen knew that underneath that tough exterior, he was a soft and affectionate person. He had seen how it hurt him if Kishen got even a slight scratch on his body. No, Kishen should have behaved himself. In future he would remember not to trouble him ever again.

But would he compromise and not attend Daataa Anand's hearing in Justice Shankar's court? Kishen had no hold over himself in this regard.

11

Daataa Anand had a firm hand on the pulse of his followers. He comprehended instinctively that basically, they all wanted to run away from their miseries and problems. They all wanted freedom from their responsibilities. He made use of this observation to form the base of his religious philosophy.

He would advise his followers to shun all worldly bondage, ignore the powerful human need for the approval of friends and relatives. He told his followers that these were the factors in life which unnecessarily bound them to duty and obligations. He would emphasize that there was just one everlasting relationship that needed to be built and sustained, and that was with god. 'God is the only one who can make you eternally happy. He is yours; love him with all your heart and soul. And the only person who can help you see god, give you the pleasure to feel him, converse with him, embrace him, is your guru. So have faith in your guru, surrender your complete self to your guru, love him, give him your heart, mind and soul, and see how you are transported to a divine realm. You will experience happiness like never before and you will maintain that state of bliss and happiness till the end of your life. And that is what life is meant for. God wants you to be happy, so be happy, sing and dance with joy—life is 'Anandam hi anandam . . .'

No matter how easy he made it all seem, the fact is that it is not child's play to overcome the complexities of life. Human egos are like monsters who want supremacy over all others. There is competition in degrees of happiness too. Every person wants to be happier than the other. We like to believe that we are the best. Our friends and relatives doing better than us is a perennial cause of our heartburn and suffering. People begin to pity themselves when their close ones earn more, live lavishly. 'How can god be so partial? How can he give them so much and nothing to us?' they ask, perplexed. And thus it is easy for even a half-intelligent man to entrap and rule over these jealous, vulnerable souls simply by bringing them under his seemingly loving and caring protection. The disciples, in turn, remain indebted to the omniscient guru forever, and blindly follow what he preaches.

The nature of problems seems to be very different in Western countries. In the West, the problem is one of rampant impermanence, especially where relationships are concerned. It is as if, with changing seasons, relationships are changed too to suit the latest trends. And when people get bored and fed up of changing their house, car, fridge, life partner, they look for something entirely different and more exciting. And it is at that point gurus like Daataa Anand come in handy.

The foreigners were so impressed with Daataa's discourses that they did not think twice before selling off their houses, businesses, properties and joining him. Money does not make one happy, and it was not required for their new found, spiritually rich and happy lifestyle. So they gave generously to Daataa's well-spread charity net and joined in his religious opera: 'Anandam hi anandam'.

Daataa became a rich person in no time. His cash box overflowed with crisp currency notes. And since he could not handle his finances alone, he made his very close friend Rehmat his secretary-cum-accountant. Rehmat was trustworthy, faithful and competent. Moreover, he was Rachna's rakhi brother and protector in her difficult days.

As time progressed, Daataa's bank account swelled. He had never seen so much money ever in his life, nor had he ever dreamt of becoming so rich. He lost faith and became suspicious of close associates like Rehmat. He would question him on every issue, every transaction, every account. Rehmat found it humiliating. Mutual trust was lost and there was a lot of tension between the two. Rehmat did not like Daataa's falling moral standards and Daataa developed doubts about Rehmat's integrity. And even as all this happened, Rachna know nothing of these tensions.

One day, Daataa and Rehmat had a major showdown. Rehmat disappeared after that. Daataa told Rachna that he had to send Rehmat to Arizona to take charge of that end of the organization. Daataa had no one in his ashram who came from that side of America, so he knew that no one would be able to find him and his secret would be safe.

Rachna sent many letters to Rehmat at the address Daataa had given her, but received no reply. There were no mobiles or the Internet during those days. There was a telephone number, though. Rachna would book a trunk call to the number and keep waiting for days together, but Rehmat never answered. Rachna got worried. She started wondering. Was there something wrong? Why should Daataa give her a wrong address and telephone number? What could the reason be? But she never received convincing answers to any of her questions. Why was Daataa hiding facts from her? What had happened between the two? Something was definitely not right. Rachna's mind was full of questions and she felt her trust had been betrayed by the man who had professed to love her forever.

12

'This case is unnecessarily wasting the High Court's precious time. God knows what Justice Shankar is trying to prove! Why can't he just wrap it up quickly and give a judgement?' Mr Das said to his son, expecting a reaction. There was none. Mr Das picked up a copy of the *Indian Nation*, the morning newspaper, and continued, 'Another eyewitness turns hostile. Says he had been pressurized to say what he said earlier. This is the headline today.'

Kishen did not comment. His father went on, 'I wonder why Justice Shankar is so adamant! God knows what he is trying to do. And such arrogance! Perhaps he suffers from some kind of complex. Wants everything his way. Can you believe it, he even refused to go to the airport to receive Madam! As if it was below his dignity to show respect to the great lady. He will learn his lesson the hard way if he does not change his attitude!'

Kishen Das was amused. This was the first time that his father had opened up on this topic with him. He smiled. 'Papa, cool it! Justice Shankar's stance is his lookout. Why do I feel as if you are jealous of him? Not because he is my ideal, my hero, but somewhere, deep within your heart, you also want to revolt against the Emergency like Judge Saab and not obey unreasonable orders from the supreme command! Unfortunately, you are a government officer directly under her rule, and you do realize that you will be taken to task the moment you open your mouth. Why just you, I think 90 per cent of the government servants, if they did not fear losing their jobs, would cry hoarse against this atrocious government. But when you know that it is not possible, what else can you do except find fault with this brave man?' Kishen Das had hit the bullseye.

'You should be ashamed of yourself for talking like this with your father. What has the world come to? We gave so much respect to our parents. My father's words were pure wisdom, never to be questioned. It was considered the height of bad manners to voice one's opinions against his comments. And here you are, a member of the know-it-all generation, with no sense of values, thinking that their elders are big fools. No regard for age and experience. Just say any damn thing that comes to your mind. Shocking!' He threw the paper in Kishen's direction and got up.

All this high-voltage drama was an everyday affair. Kishen was so used to it that all he did was reply, 'All right, Papa, you think that Justice Shankar is taking it a bit too far, but do you know all that Daataa Anand has done? You only take away someone's life when you kill, but his crime is much greater than that. Do you have any idea how he has crushed innocent souls? You will not be able to imagine the way he has tortured some of his own people before killing them. You will not be able to hear about it, it so gruesome!'

'Who told you all this?'

Kishen went blank for a while and then wondered, indeed, who could have told him all this? Maybe he had read something like this in the newspapers, but try as he might, he could not recollect the source of this information. He was intrigued. What had made him so sure that he was telling the truth? Did he have any proof? Kishen was puzzled. His head began to throb, his neck began to get stiff. Was he about to have another attack of his undiagnosed disease?

His father interjected, 'Anyway, the doctor has asked you to see him today. Perhaps he will take a CAT scan. Come to my office in the evening at four. Ask the Secretariat guards to inform me as soon as you reach there. I will come down and we will go straight to his clinic. And mind you, four sharp is the time. Don't make me wait like you make poor Seema wait!'

Kishen just nodded his head to say 'okay'. He understood why his father emphasized punctuality. He smiled—he did not have to go to the court that day, so there was no problem in reaching his father's office.

He knew his father still did not consider him adult enough to go to the doctor alone. Had his mother been alive, things would have been different. But in her absence, Mr Das took his responsibilities very seriously.

Dialogues with his father were a novelty for Kishen. He did not remember being close to him at all when his mother was alive. She had died of cancer when he was just about five. Kishen's earliest memories of his father were that of a grim, overly busy man who brought work home every day. They hardly ever sat together and talked or laughed or went out to the market together, or visited friends and relatives. His mother would go alone with him even for parent–teacher meetings. Kishen was often jealous of his friends whose fathers accompanied them. But his mother more than made up for his father's absence. Going out on holidays together as a family was a dream that Kishen could never fulfill. The only holidays he had were the visits to his grandparents who lived in their village Simri in Darbhanga in north Bihar. There, too, he went mostly with his mother during vacations, and he loved playing with the village lads in the open fields, screaming, singing, whistling and gurgling with laughter over the simplest things, not burdened with studies and school discipline. Left to his devices, Kishen would have loved to permanently settle in Simri. His father detested the village. He failed to understand his son's affinity with those urchins and so Mr Das would often chide Kishen or tell his mother sternly that she was spoiling him rotten. He wanted Kishen to study hard during the holidays and always come first in the exams. He often told his mother that Kishen had to become an officer like him and join the IAS. And even as his father said those words, Kishen firmly made up his mind against it.

13

Daataa Anand had figured out a novel method to please his followers and keep them satisfied. He thus trapped them so firmly in his net that they were unable to find their way out. The disciples staying in his ashram were given time to meet him individually in his room. The interaction was on a one-to-one basis and the matters discussed were of a confidential and private nature. Daataa would probe with great diligence to find whatever it was that ailed his disciples. Then they would try to find a solution together. Sometimes, even if no solution seemed forthcoming, it helped to get the pain out of their system by just confiding in their esteemed guru.

Daataa was at his compassionate best on such occasions. And the exercise worked both ways. His disciples were happy that they got special attention, that he showed personal interest in them and made them feel good and confident about themselves. It helped them get over their depression and other sorrows. And as for Daataa, this was a great opportunity to cement his hold on his disciples. He now knew their pressure points, the things that made them vulnerable, their little secrets.

Daataa could hypnotize his disciples completely with honeyed, emotional talk. People completely overcame their inhibitions in front of him and would surrender their mind, body, their entire being, at his feet. The devotees, specially the young girls, were so charmed that they were ready to do whatever Daataa asked them to do. Lack of experience and wisdom made them feel as if they were serving god himself. He became like an uncrowned emperor, or even higher than that, he became god almighty!

Fame and money achieved at an early age had corrupted Daataa utterly. And little did he realize that lust, an inflated ego and arrogance were pushing him towards defeat and destruction. His position, his wealth, his followers, his wisdom, his righteousness, Daataa took everything for granted. For him at that time, life was at his beck and call. He could influence and mould people any way he wanted to—Daataa felt all-powerful.

There were any number of Rachnas now ready to please and serve Daataa. He just had to make his wish known and they would be more than eager to come to his room any time of the day or night. He would make love to them, dance with them, explain and demonstrate various kinds of anandam. He had full control and all the privileges over the hearts, minds, bodies and souls of these unsuspecting naïve girls. Daataa's call was like god's special command to them. There was no limit to the kind of services they were ready and happy to provide for their lord. They were constantly told that giving solace, comfort and pleasure to Daataa was the highest form of devotion possible. And, in return, Daataa would bless them, help them, and give them all that they asked for.

All that Daataa had read earlier about Swami Vivekanand and his lofty philosophies was conveniently forgotten. He had travelled too far and in too opposite a direction from the destination he had sought at the beginning of his journey. The ideologies he started with, too, morphed and began to focus exclusively on the idea of today. Daataa now propagated the idea of living like there was no tomorrow. 'The time to live and be happy is now, so live it up. Don't just exist—live life king-size. God wants you to be happy, content and grateful to him for all that he has bestowed upon you. Don't disappoint and insult him with your woes and frustrations. Dance to *Anandam hi anandam* with love, energy and passion. That is what we have come to this earth for.'

Meanwhile, Rachna gave birth to Daataa's son. She threatened that she would take the child to Hazaribagh, to his mother, if Daataa did not marry her. Daataa did not want even a whiff of scandal to be associated with him so he quickly caught hold of a priest, took Rachna to a faraway temple and solemnized their marriage in front of two of his trustworthy lieutenants. But there was one condition he had imposed on Rachna: there was no way she could live with him in the ashram. If his mother arrived unannounced, what would he tell her? He bought Rachna a sprawling bungalow on the bank of the river Ganga in Chandernagore.

For Daataa, his mother was just an excuse. In fact, he did not want Rachna to be an obstruction in his scheme of things. His old mother was not able to move about because of arthritis. Her able son had bought her the same old house in Hazaribagh where she had brought the newly born Anurag. He had also employed a number of servants and maids to take care of her. He had personally supervised arrangements and seen to it that his mother was comfortable. He used to visit her every now and then. After all, she was almost the only person he really had regard for and whom he worshipped.

The mother was more than grateful to god for giving her such a caring, obedient and dutiful son. He was so compassionate and kind and she could never find enough words to praise him. No other son could compare with him. But Rachna was now beginning to understand and question a lot of things. Why could she not meet his mother? Why could she not live with him in his ashram? Things were not all that simple. Rehmat never returned from Arizona. The two eyewitnesses to their wedding, too, suddenly disappeared. Rachna's misgivings only grew. But Daataa Anand often visited and talked to her so sweetly and so convincingly that she would feel guilty for entertaining such treacherous thoughts in her mind. However, one night, something very strange happened.

Daataa had come to Chandernagore. When Rachana woke up at night, Daataa was missing. She searched for him all over but he was nowhere to be found. She waited for him for some time, and then, just as she was dozing off, she saw something very scary. A man wearing a black robe, with two large bones in one hand, a skull in the other, a broad vermilion mark across his forehead, his eyes bloodshot and a queer expression on his face, entered the room. Once inside, he began prancing about in a frenzy. Rachna was so afraid, she fainted. But in the morning, she saw Daataa sleeping peacefully on his side of the bed with a smile on his lips. There was no change in him; he looked absolutely normal. Rachna asked him where he was during the night.

Daata replied with a smile, 'Where would I go? I was sleeping peacefully. I must say this house has something special. I feel so relaxed here. I think it is you who makes all the difference. You are god's best gift to me, Rachna!' He took her in his arms and then said, 'On the contrary, I saw you searching for something at night! What happened? What were you looking for?'

Rachna was stumped. He was speaking so confidently that she got confused. Was it a hallucination? Could it have been a nightmare? Who was that man she had seen? He had looked just like Daataa! Rachna's confusion took on giant proportions. Was she imagining things? And then, when her son turned two, Daataa disappeared one night along with him. She looked all over for the two of them and nearly became hysterical. Then she opened the windows of her bedroom and saw a weird scene. She saw Daataa meditating next to the river with his eyes closed. Their son lay right in front of him in deep slumber. But everything was back to normal in the morning, as if nobody had ever moved at all.

Rachna was going crazy; she felt as if she was losing her mind. She did not trust herself any more, she found her husband mysterious, and she did not know what was happening to her son. She prayed fervently, 'God! What is all this? Help me understand all this, please!'

14

The telephone rang at Justice Shankar's residence. Meera, his wife, picked it up. An unknown voice informed her that he was a well-wisher of Justice Shankar's. He just wanted to tell her that Judge Saab's life was in danger. He should be careful. Some people were making plans to assassinate him. They were dangerous people and fully capable of executing their plans.

'People know about Judge Saab's punctuality,' added the well-wisher. 'It would be safer if he could keep changing his time schedule. It would help upset their plans.'

When Meera asked for a name, the man did not reply. He only said, 'I will show up at an appropriate time, ma'am. For the time being I just wanted to say that in my own small way, I am also giving Judge Saab protection. My inner soul tells me that Justice Shankar has to be saved at all costs.' Before disconnecting, he said that he would alert them in case he got to know about the moves of the enemy.

Meera wanted to ask more questions but the call was disconnected. She kept wondering: Who is he? Why was he so concerned about Justice Shankar's safety? Was he in any way connected with Daataa Anand's case? But the man had hung up. There was no way to find out.

After disconnecting the phone, Kishen Das delved deep into his own thoughts. He was unable to analyse why he felt this compelling desire to save Justice Shankar. Nevertheless, he had taken the lead, collected his moral strength, picked up the flag of determination and made the call. He was very sure that he was not alone, very soon there would be a convoy of like-minded people following him in the pursuit of truth and justice.

After hanging up, Meera felt miserable and depressed. Life was becoming tough for Justice Shankar and his family. Their son Aditya had been hit on Fraser Road by a speeding jeep only a few days ago. He fell from his bike, unconscious, and heard a few voices in the crowd identifying him, 'Oh! Justice Shankar's son, Aditya?' but no one came to his rescue.

Just the other day, even the strong-willed Justice Shankar had almost crumbled when his daughter Mona had called up from Delhi, hysterical and sobbing, unable to speak. Her son was not in the school bus when it returned in the afternoon to drop the children home. She imagined the worst as they had received threatening calls just the day before. She pleaded with her father to get the Daataa case transferred to some other bench or resign.

Justice Shankar thought for a while, then picked up the phone and dialled the number of the commissioner of police in Delhi who happened to be his friend. He updated him on the situation and asked for his advice. The commissioner promised that he would do the needful and revert back to the judge immediately.

Justice Shankar sat still, motionless, fed up with life and the deplorable state of affairs. Rather disillusioned with his principles and views, his faith shaken, he waited for a call from the commissioner. Meanwhile, he kept debating with himself, should I resign and accept defeat? Disappoint and fail all those who had pinned their hopes on me? What should I do?

Meera often found herself wishing that her husband had not taken up Daataa Anand's case. She liked thinking about the days when her husband was not a judge in the High Court. Her family was so carefree and safe those days! What was the point of challenging such a powerful chief of a notorious religious gang? They had the money to buy people over. They were ready to do anything at all to save Daataa Anand. They shamelessly bribed everyone, from an ordinary peon to the highest authorities, to win the case. How could Justice Shankar fight such a battle alone? He needed evidence to prove Daataa guilty. Would the dishonest officers and concerned people change their mind and tell the truth? Would they support him just because he was bravely venturing on to a path full of thorns alone? Times had changed. The balance tilted more towards money rather than truth. The people who had been killed were simple, trusting and ordinary—who would stand up for them? Their own family members would rather utilize the opportunity to become rich by selling their souls. The dead were not going to come back, so why worry about right and wrong? Meera knew that this was a hopeless situation, but she decided to keep her thoughts and opinions to herself and support her husband whole-heartedly and with courage. They were both trying to put up a brave front when Mona called again. She was very relieved and informed them that her son had been found. The boy had been sleeping in his bus, hence missed his bus-stop and that had created all the commotion and suspense. Justice Shankar heaved a sigh of relief and thanked god. Then he talked to Mona, admonishing her lightly for her immature reaction, 'I am ready and willing to step down for your happiness and peace of mind, but don't forget, this will only encourage the evil elements of society. Today they are just threatening, tomorrow they will openly show off and brandish their guns and weapons out on the roads to scare people and bully them. My life is at its fag end, tomorrow you people will have to face it all. If these threats and vandalism are not stopped today, then very soon this country will be run by cheats and criminals. The law and constitution will find its place only in history and money and might will rule. There will be new Hitlers in every state of our country, running their offices at gunpoint!'

'But that is already happening, Babuji. I did not want to tell you this, but you know, two strangers came to our house two days ago, introduced themselves as our distant relatives from our village, and tried to tell us you should favour Daataa Anand because the guru is a spiritual person and innocent. He has a huge following. If his disciples were hurt by a wrong judgement, they could create hell for you. And when Amit showed them the door, they made sure that Amit noticed the pistols in their pockets. They warned us that we should take care of Sandeep.' Mona broke down again.

Even though Daataa Anand's threats stood on one side and the baton of the Emergency dangled on the other, Justice Shankar held fort. It was not easy at all, but he had learnt to be brave and enjoy dealing with dangerous situations right from his childhood. Justice Shankar's father had been a harsh disciplinarian. He would never approve of his son bunking school, classes and studies to run from one village to the other, delivering secret letters to freedom fighters. Little Shankar was just eight years old when he jumped into the freedom struggle along with his grandfather. His father thought it was all futile, nothing would come of it, so he would be livid, scold him and beat him. But little Shankar would take it all in good spirit—his motherland needed him, and he had to contribute his bit; that was all that mattered. His patriotism, in its purest form at that young age, was at its zenith. He was truly devoted to his grandfather and felt proud to run errands for him. His grandfather would often tell him stories about the atrocities of the British, and how a revolution had taken shape under the leadership of people like Mahatma Gandhi. Little Shankar would listen to him spellbound. Acting with full responsibility, he would hide important letters inside his textbooks. And if any policeman expressed doubts, he would very confidently push the book under the policeman's nose and ask him to take a look. His confidence did the trick—it fooled the policemen and they would let him go. He often felt and was quite certain that his grandfather and he, by themselves, were strong enough to drive the British away and free the motherland from slavery.

A patriot is born under such circumstances. The strength of character, the determination, the will to fight the wrong and the unjust—all of this shapes a man right from his childhood. And it is this kind of background that produces a bold and fearless judge like Justice Shankar who does his duty with full honesty and does not care at all even if he has to deliver a judgement against the authority in power.

Justice Shankar declared, 'A man does not die or come back to life by shouting slogans like "murdabad" or "zindabad". So many students who are put behind bars for merely raising such slogans have committed no crime and, therefore, they do not require bail. They should be set free.'

His judgement was celebrated inside and outside the jail with a full-throated, 'Justice Shankar zindabad!' The students guided by Jaiprakash Narain were in full force outside the jail to receive their friends who were now free and there was much jubilation.

This was considered a great victory for the rebels protesting against the Emergency. Justice Shankar had dared to hold the judiciary's and his own head high at a time when even the Supreme Court had meekly bowed down. Although it was a very small, insignificant judgement, it was an act of courage and an assertion of bold defiance against the ruling despots.

Justice Shankar's popularity was soaring and Madam's chamchas were worried. It hardly made a difference to the throne, but the chamchas would spice up their reports to the high command. Judge Saab never had any high aspirations nor did he intend to threaten the mighty seat of power, but when the high and mighty supreme leader heard the exaggerated version, she got worked up.

Just as Don Quixote tried to defeat the windmill with his sword, the chamchas began attempts to cut down Justice Shankar to size. They devised ways to have him transferred to some bureaucratic backwater, but failed. After that they tried to lure him with a Rajya Sabha membership. They said that there wasn't a better nominee from Bihar. If Justice Shankar would give his consent, then the membership was his for asking.

Justice Shankar replied that he did not have such ambitions; he was quite happy with what he had. There were any number of capable people who should be given a chance to attend the Rajya Sabha. He very well understood the meaning of such favours—if you want to control someone, oblige him to such an extent that he will start toeing your line.

Justice Shankar was not easy to corner. The drive to shunt him out turned into a game of chess: the queen on one side and the king on the other, yet the pawn found ways to save itself. The loyalty for his country, his love and passion for the motherland was still strong, but Justice Shankar was now rather disheartened with the deteriorating conditions, the corruption, the falling standards. Whenever he felt low, his grandfather's image flashed across his mind. He would remember what his grandfather used to say, 'Conditions are not going to be easy even if we get independence, son. We have tackled our share of the storm, it is your turn now. Face it with all your might and never stray from the path of truth.' And this gave Justice Shankar the courage to march forward fearlessly.

15

Justice Shankar treated all his friends and relatives with love and care. He was a man who touched each life with special charm and made everyone feel like they had a special corner in his heart. He had this unique way of dealing with his fellow beings that made them feel important, as if he loved each more than he loved the other. His company was relaxing, soothing and cherished by all who came in contact with him. People flooded his house, enjoyed being with him and basked in his warm hospitality. But the guards stationed outside his house found this problematic. Every day they would come across new people who would claim that they were Justice Shankar's closest relatives or friends.

One evening Judge Saab was not feeling too well. He had slight fever. And whoever heard about it headed straight to his house. Eight to ten people had already arrived. The guards were also quite fed up checking so many of them.

And then, Justice Shankar's nephew Dr. Sharan arrived. A busy and famous senior doctor at the Patna Medical College and Hospital, he did not see the guards at the gate, turned inside and drove past them at full speed. One of the guards came charging, pointed his gun directly at the front window, and screamed, 'Stop right now!'

The doctor was taken aback. Nervous and speechless, he stepped out of the car with both his arms up. The guard then put the barrel of the gun on his chest and shouted, 'Who are you?'

The young doctor's vocal cords refused to flutter out of tension and fright. Just then Judge Saab's five-year-old grandson Rahul heard the commotion and ran to the scene. He shouted, 'Friend! Friend!' and ran as fast as he could to his uncle and clasped his arms around his legs. The guard put his gun down after the identity of the newcomer was established.

Rahul escorted the doctor to his nana's room. His excitement level was at its peak—there was so much to narrate to his nana. Justice Shankar was very upset to hear what had happened. He said, 'All those who come to my house are my own people, either my relatives or my friends, certainly not my enemies. Can't they understand that? I don't want these security guards stopping people. No, earlier also I had objected to having them around, and now I am very sure they will have to go. I don't want them pointing guns at my dear ones. They make me feel small.' The judge was almost in tears. But Dr Sharan did not think that it was the guard's fault; he was just doing his duty.

Dr Sharan tried to explain the guard's stance again because he felt that Justice Shankar needed the protection of the guards. 'No, no, Mamu. In fact, they got suspicious because I drove in so fast. It was completely my fault.'

Judge Saab replied, 'Son, isn't that the normal way to drive when you are entering your own house? I don't want to live in a jail, with them watching all of us all the time.'

'But Mamu, you need protection,' Dr Sharan said.

'My protector, my saviour, is up there, looking down at me from the sky. If he wants to call me up, all these armed men will keep holding their guns and I will go. Who are they to protect me? Tomorrow morning, I must ring up the registrar and ask him to dismantle this useless security net and end this circus.'

Justice Shankar's younger daughter Rajani had come to visit her parents for a short while. The next day, her son was turning five. His birthday gift, a cycle, had to be bought. Rahul was adamant that he wanted his gift that very same day. When he started howling, his nana intervened, and he got his gift a day earlier. It made him so happy that he would not stop thanking Nana the whole day. 'Nana, you are my best friend, my angel, the best nana in the whole world!'

He was learning to balance his bike near the portico outside. The old servant Birju was teaching him Rahul was a friendly child and a non-stop chatterbox. All the servants, peons, driver, gardener, the battery of guards were his friends. He enjoyed chatting, laughing, playing, joking with them all the time. When he came close to the outside gate, the armed guard standing there saluted him. Rahul also replied with a salute, smiled and said, 'Hey, Mr Policeman! Yesterday you almost took away my mamu's life. Why were you shooting him with your gun? Now you will have to answer to my nana. He is going to dismiss all of you. So start packing.'

One of the guards standing close by could not believe his ears. He came running after Rahul and tried to replace Birju and hold the cycle. Rahul shouted, 'No, no, you leave it, Mr Policeman! You yourself don't know how to cycle, what will you teach me?' Rahul laughed. 'I saw you the other day, trying to learn, and diving into the open drains outside the gate along with your cycle! Did you enjoy the splash in that stinking water? And did the frogs bite you?'

The guard ignored all that Rahul had said. 'Oh, you saw me that day? Yes I was learning but now I have become an expert and can beat anybody in cycle racing.'

'Really!' Rahul seemed impressed.

'What were you saying, Babu? Who is being dismissed?'

Rahul felt important. He was carrying news that none of these people knew. He was happy with himself. He laughed and said, 'All of you. Nana says all of you are quite useless.'

The guard looked worried. He had still not performed the task he was sent here for. He would have to take action fast before the guards were packed off.

Not enough time, he thought, if they remove us from here; then money will again become scarce. How will I survive just on the salary? The fat envelope coming every month from Daataa Anand will stop, I must do something alarming so that Justice Shankar has no option but to let us continue. But what can I do? The guard's thought process stretched out its wings and began to soar. He kept planning the whole night. Around 3 a.m., he got a bright idea. His duty was till 9 a.m., after which another guard would replace him. Quietly he got up and disappeared without informing anybody. Patna was a small town, one could easily go up to any other corner of the city and return within two hours. He picked up his cycle and raced to his destination.

The guard returned and took his position at the crack of dawn. Nobody had any idea that he had been missing for two and a half hours. The sentry on duty at the gate was sleeping—his head would tumble left to right, up and down, and every now and then he would wake up with a start. This suited the other guard. He offered to do his duty and sent the sentry to take a nap.

Judge Saab had an inkling that all was not well. Whatever threats they were getting, the address of his daughter in Delhi, the inside information, was all passed on by these supposedly faithful guards. And now he even wondered if these guards had a hand in putting that horrible letter in his file, the one that he got in his courtroom the other day! No, his personal staff was loyal, it was these guards that he did not trust any more. The next morning the registrar got a telephone call at about 9.30 a.m., instructing him to make arrangements to remove the security guards from Justice Shankar's residence.

16

Kishen Das did not only worry about Justice Shankar's safety. He went a step ahead by taking concrete action and forming an information network to gather all possible details about preparations being made by the enemy camp. He made friends with various people who could come handy in various situations. They formed a group of 'well-wishers'. Thus his network covered arms dealers, employees in explosives and ammunition factories and wrestlers' arenas on one side. Police posts, police officers, guards on night vigil as well as bank officials were also in his network. He had also made friends with some vegetable and fruit vendors who used to roam around Daataa Anand's ashram. He had requested them all to inform him at once if they heard anything suspicious. All his friends had high regard for Justice Shankar and they were quite alert all the time.

That particular day Kishen left home early. He had to make

up with Seema for not turning up at her college again. Both of them were happily having a breakfast of puri and jalebi at the Marwari Basa, their favourite restaurant. In fact, of late, Kishen had been so busy with the court case that he had not spent much time with Seema and she was very upset with him. When Kishen rang her up to apologize, she had disconnected without saying anything. Kishen understood immediately that this time he had stretched it a bit too far. Seema was a sweet and understanding kind of a person. She would usually give him a chance to explain, but this time she was obviously hurt beyond words. However, Kishen knew how to be contrite and make his girl happy, so the morning saw him up before time and heading straight to Seema's house. When she opened the door, Kishen smiled. Seema did not respond.

'I couldn't sleep last night, Seema! I have been thinking only about you!' he pleaded.

'Liar!' Seema turned away.

'Say that again! You look ravishing with that expression.'

'So what have you come here for? You want me to give you sleeping pills?' Seema had asked rudely, ignoring Kishen's flattery.

'I have come here to soothe my burning eyes. I just want to look at you.'

'Shut up! Don't I know you?'

'You do? Come, tell me all that you know about me and give me a chance to defend myself, we are going out for breakfast,' Kishen spoke in one breath and pulled her on to his motorbike.

'Wait, I need to inform my family,' Seema said, knowing that Kishan would not take 'no' for an answer.

Kishen thought this was the best way to get through to her. They spent an hour dealing with every issue, however small, concerning their relationship and in the end, they smiled at each other, held hands, and made promises of everlasting love, care, trust and friendship. All faults were forgiven and forgotten.

Refuelled and brimming with fresh energy, Kishen dropped Seema back and headed home. Even from a distance he could see that his father was angry. He had come out without informing him and his father did not like his authority being taken for granted. But as he came closer, he realized that Mr Das was more worried than angry.

The moment Kishen drove in, his father vented his feelings. 'Didn't I tell you yesterday that we have an appointment with the doctor at 10.30? And here you are, just not concerned! No sense of timing, priorities, useless boy! What was the urgency to go out so early in the morning? And that, too, without informing me? Where and why did you go?'

'I remember about the appointment, Papa. Let's go,' Kishen replied very calmly.

Mr Das was still walking up and down, furious with his son. 'And so many telephone calls since morning. When I asked who was speaking, he did not give the name. What did he say?' Mr Das thought for a while and said, 'Yes, "well-wisher". He said tell him a well-wisher called. As if the rest of the world is your enemy . . . he alone cares for you . . . What kind of friends are these? Stupid fools! Well-wisher indeed!'

Kishen perked up. 'Well-wisher' was their code word! 'Did you note down the telephone number?' he enquired urgently, running inside the house towards the telephone.

Without looking at Kishen, a still annoyed Mr Das replied, 'It is lying next to the telephone, but please tell your "well-wisher",' he pronounced the word emphasizing every syllable, 'that you have to go to the hospital. It is getting late.'

Before Kishen could pick up the receiver to dial the number, it rang again.

Kishen was listening very intently; somebody was giving him information that last night one of the guards deputed at Justice Shankar's residence had gone to the ammunition factory, given some money to the guard and taken away some explosives.

Kishen Das was extremely apprehensive now. What did the guard plan to do? He looked at his watch; it was two minutes past 10 a.m. He dialled Justice Shankar's residence. The peon responded, 'Judge Saab is already in the car, going to the court. Please call him up in his office after fifteen minutes.'

'But this is very urgent, if you could . . .'

But the peon had disconnected. Kishen thought he heard a loud bang just as the line got disconnected, but he told himself it was his imagination. He only sighed and hung up. He was getting all worked up and didn't know what to do. If only Judge Saab had heeded his request and changed his office timings!

His father was reminding him every now and then that it was getting late. It was already 10.15 a.m. Kishen had no option. He would be able to plan out a course of action only after returning from the hospital. Deep in thought, he sat in the car. Just as they came out to the main road, his father asked, 'So, what was your well-wisher saying?'

'Nothing,' Kishen said, not wanting to tell anything to his father because he knew he wouldn't understand.

'Oh! So he rang up so many times to say nothing? Very funny! Such great well-wishers you have, who say nothing to you and make me run in and out so many times, as if giving me practice for some national games! Great!'

Kishen Das was in no mood to talk to his father. All this while he was only thinking and worrying about his hero, Justice Shankar. He was praying for his safety all along. He was pleading with god to shield Justice Shankar from all evils, accidents and mishaps, bullets, bombs—anything that could harm him.

At the same time, he was frustrated that he had to visit the doctor at this crucial juncture and kept murmuring, 'Why did the doctor have to call me today?'

Mr Das was even more puzzled with his son's disturbed state. He did not like Kishen's secretive attitude on the matter. 'Stupid fellow! He doesn't know his father's powers. I can solve his problems in a jiffy,' he said to himself. At the same time, he was happy that at least the doctor would now be able to step in and find a cure for Kishen.

17

In spite of the well-wisher's warning, Justice Shankar remained punctual. How could he change his office timings because of some stupid threat? He would stick to his schedule of sitting in the car exactly at 10 a.m. every day to leave for his office.

Patna High Court was just about a twelve-minute drive from his home. In those days, the roads were not congested, the population being much less than it is today. Just as he was about to sit in the car, Rahul came running and caught hold of his nana's hands. It was his birthday and he wanted to stop Nana from going to the court. Nana kissed him and very affectionately assured him that he would return early, and then they would play carom in the evening. But Rahul did not relent. He quickly ran to the other side and got into the car with the judge. 'If you don't listen to me, then I will also come with you to your school,' Rahul was very firm about his decision.

Justice Shankar smiled at the child's innocence and said, 'My teacher is very strict and you have not worn your shoes. What if she scolds and punishes us both?' Rahul looked at his bare feet, made a sour face and made his nana promise that he would come back definitely by 3 p.m. Nana agreed.

Still sulking, Rahul reluctantly stepped out of the car. Just as he banged the door shut, there were three earth-shaking blasts at the gate. The sounds reverberated with the intensity of an earthquake. The car shook and jumped a little. Rahul fell down, his whole body shaken by the sudden impact, screaming and crying with terror. He had scratches on his hands and feet and they started bleeding. For a second even Justice Shankar became dizzy, trying to figure out what had happened. He jumped out of the car and looked at the gate. A huge column of smoke enveloped the gate area.

The guard who had joined his duty at the gate just half an hour earlier was lying on the road, unconscious. The order to have the guards removed from duty at the judge's bungalow had not yet come into effect.

All this sudden burst of noise—the blast, the crying and the screaming—brought everyone to the portico. They were all speaking together about how they heard the ear-shattering sound, what they thought had happened and how they had left everything that they were doing and came out. Rajani was in the bath. She thought the guard had aimed the gun at Rahul as he was still crying very loudly. But the sound she had heard was more like an explosion. Something very serious had happened. She pulled on a dressing gown and charged down madly.

By the time she reached Rahul, Meera had already picked him up and was trying to pacify him. One look at Rahul and Rajani heaved a sigh of relief. She took him in her arms, hugged him close, and when she saw his bleeding wounds, started sobbing. Tears rolling down freely on her cheeks, she kept questioning her parents, 'What happened?'

Everyone was asking each other, 'What happened?'

Only Meera and Justice Shankar had understood by now that if Rahul had not stopped Justice Shankar with his innocent pleas, and if the judge had left on time like always, he would have been blown up along with his car. This was a murder attempt.

Their old servant Birju was unable to grasp all that had happened just now. He went blank for a while, but it soon dawned on him that someone had tried to kill his master. He came up to Judge Saab and with folded hands started speaking, 'Sir, today I will offer sweets to the almighty for saving your life. This was an attempt to kill you. I will not leave the person who tried to do this to you. Only a mad person would think of taking your life. The day I come to know who has done this, I will slit his throat.' Saying this, Birju started sobbing.

Judge Saab put his hands around Birju's shoulder, trying to calm him down. He asked his driver to put the unconscious guard in his car and take him straight to the hospital. Another guard was also sent along to help him. He called up his nephew Dr Sharan and told him about the incident and asked him to have the guard attended to urgently. He asked him not to wait for the police formalities as a life was in danger. The police formalities could be taken care of later.

Justice Shankar called up the registrar to inform him that he would be a little late. When he explained the situation, the registrar instantly said he was coming at once and an FIR would have to be lodged immediately. One call to the registrar was enough for the news to spread like wild fire. The entire court learnt it in no time and they informed their near and dear ones. Subsequently, the telephone started ringing endlessly at the judge's residence. Whoever could come was on his way to Strand Road.

Birju went up to the gate to assess the damage. Suddenly, he spotted a bundle of blood-soaked clothes. As he went close, he saw a man lying face down, bleeding profusely. Birju called out to the judge, 'Sir, there is one lying here too!'

Meera tried to stop him, but her husband thought it was his responsibility and duty to look after his people. As he came close to Birju, Birju turned the man face up and gasped, 'Maali!' His face was burnt, but he was still recognizable.

The maali, the gardener, was poor. He was not as old as he looked. Poverty, problems and responsibility had aged him much before his time. His wife was suffering from various diseases and the judge used to give him money for her treatment. Sometimes, he used to ask his nephew to treat the woman for free.

The judge thought that the maali's untimely death had freed him from his plight, but saddled his ten-year-old son with responsibilities too gigantic for his frail shoulders. The son was a bright student and used to dream of becoming a well-respected man himself—like a judge, one day. One blast had shattered his dreams and his future to pieces. The judge's head bowed in grief. The gardener had paid a heavy price for being with him. But life goes on, it does not wait for anyone to pause, take a deep breath and to prepare oneself to face a new tomorrow.

18

'Why did we have to come so early? We are wasting precious time sitting in this dim, suffocating, wretched corridor? The doctor has not even arrived yet! God knows when he will come!' Kishen was mightily irritated. Justice Shankar's guard collecting explosives from the factory at night was a frightening development. The 'well-wisher's gang' would have to act immediately and abort the dangerous schemes of the enemy. This was a real emergency and here he was, unnecessarily trapped in the hospital. Impatient, he got up. 'Papa! It's so stuffy here! Please fix up an appointment for another day, I am going, I have important . . .'

Mr Das cut him short. 'Just who do you think you are? My boss? Just keep quiet and behave yourself. I know all about your urgent business. We had to come early because I was sick and tired of running up and down taking calls from your so-called "well-wishers",' his father retorted, still annoyed that Kishen was not including him in his little secret. Father and son were having their normal tiff as always, using their logic and common sense to hurt each other. Looking at Kishen, no one could ever say that he could be suffering from any disease. Not only did he look healthy, he was energetic, intelligent and bright in his studies and good at sports. In short, he was a normal, robust young man with a pleasant personality and agreeable disposition. Kishen Das, however, had put the local doctors in a tizzy. He had a strange ailment which the doctors were unable to diagnose. Kishen would see weird dreams and start jumping around in his sleep. At times his neck would twist with a sharp shooting pain. The pain would be so excruciating that he would restlessly roll over the floor or start running helter skelter as if he wanted to run away from himself, looking for relief—all the while still in slumber!

One he even unbolted the front door at night and sleep-walked on the roads. But he was able to remember the contents of his dreams which caused so much suffering and trauma.

His father had got a chain fixed on the door, and put a heavy lock at night for his son's safety. Whenever he got these attacks, Kishen's neck would remain stiff and hurt the whole day. Of late, the frequency of these fits had been increasing.

A number of doctors were consulted but they found nothing wrong with the young boy. He seemed in perfectly good health. His blood, urine, stool, X-ray, CAT scans, all possible tests had been found to be normal. Other alternative therapies like homeopathy, ayurveda, naturopathy had had no effect. So frustrated did Kishen's father feel that against all logical reasoning, he consulted astrologers, tantriks, practioners of black magic and others of their ilk. Strangely, Kishen's malaise seemed to defy all healing forces, whether natural or man-made.

Just as a nurse appeared at the clinic's door and called out, 'Next patient, Kishen Das,' a stretcher was wheeled into the hospital corridor. Everyone looked in that direction. It was being pushed with a great hurry towards the emergency section, making all kinds of clanking noises. Kishen Das got up and looked at the stretcher. The face was not clearly visible from where he was standing, but he saw Justice Shankar's driver running behind it. One look at the driver and Kishen fainted. Perhaps he thought that the person on the stretcher was the judge himself. This was the first time that he had fainted like this. He was also put on a stretcher immediately and wheeled into the emergency ward. At the moment Justice Shankar's nephew Dr Sharan was examining the injured guard, Kishen was being unloaded onto the bed lying next to the guard's stretcher.

Justice Shankar's guard was badly burnt and he had bled a lot too. But one very good thing about small towns is that distance is never a hindrance. He had been brought to the hospital in record time so his life could be saved. Some blood transfusion was required. His burns were treated, ointment applied, bandages tied, and after being given pain-killing injections, he was shifted to the general ward.

In the same emergency ward, a nurse was attending on Kishen Das. His blood pressure was measured, eyes checked, pulse counted and cold water applied to his forehead to bring him back to consciousness. As soon as he came to his senses, Kishen asked, 'Sister, who was on the stretcher that was just wheeled in?'

The nurse replied coolly, 'Some bomb victim with burns.'

Kishen wanted to probe further but by then the consultant appointed for him, Dr Mishra, had reached his bedside. He found Dr Sharan standing at the next bed and thought it was a good opportunity to take his advice.

Dr Mishra apprised Dr Sharan of Kishen's ailment. He read out his report and informed him that a CAT scan had also been done. Everything was clear and normal. 'His case is quite a challenge for us. He seems to be a healthy, bright young man, with no abnormality whatsoever. But this mysterious ailment has been troubling him for the past two years. What do we do? How do we treat him?'

Dr Sharan asked if a psychiatrist had been consulted.

Dr Mishra smiled. 'A psychiatrist? Well, yes, we did, but the poor man lost his own mental equilibrium. He asked me not to send such normal, confident people to him. He has not learnt to treat normal, healthy people, he said.' Dr Sharan smiled at Dr Mishra. He enjoyed such challenging cases. He asked Dr Mishra to transfer all his papers to him if he had no objections. This was exactly what Dr Mishra wanted.

Three hours later, during his lunch break, Justice Shankar came to the hospital to see the injured guard. He went to the general ward, stood next to his bed, and took the guard's hands in his own. 'You are a brave man,' said the judge.

The guard looked up at him and tried to smile, but there were bandages all over his face.

'You have a wonderful family, son, they all love you so much that as soon as they heard the news, they caught the first bus and are already on their way. They should be here any moment.'

The guard's eyes, brimming with tears, conveyed his gratitude.

'You have been working very hard for me and my family, standing out in the sun the whole day and braving the cold at night. I am truly indebted to you, but god wants you to take a little rest now. So be good and relax.'

The guard nodded his head in affirmation. He had never met Justice Shankar in person and did not know that he was such a kind gentleman. Justice Shankar patted his hand gently again, 'Don't worry, very soon you will be back on your feet. You should actually thank god that your limbs are intact. Your meals will come from my kitchen. My driver will come every day. Tell him what you would like to eat, and eat well. Your family needs you, so fight your pain for them and get well soon. All right?'

The guard was overwhelmed with emotion. He smiled weakly through his tears. And then Judge Saab took out whatever money he had in his pocket and shoved it under his pillow. 'Your family will need it,' he said, still smiling. The guard broke down again.

The police had arrived to take the guard's statement. Justice Shankar met his nephew, thanked him for his timely help and went back to the court. Justice Shankar called the registrar to his chamber and repeated his request to withdraw the guards from his house immediately. The registrar was taken aback by his decision. It was clearly written on his face that he had found this decision rather irrational.

'I beg your pardon, sir,' he said. 'I don't think I heard you correctly.' He was of the opinion that more security should now be provided to the judge. After all, an attempt had been made on his life!

'You heard exactly what I said. I don't need the security,' Justice Shankar replied in a clipped tone.

'But, sir . . .'

Justice Shankar was unyielding. Even the mention of the words 'security guards' was anathema to him and made his blood boil.

He explained his logic, 'When my relatives come, they are questioned endlessly. Guns are even aimed at them, but how is it that someone plants a bomb on my front gate and these guards keep sleeping? Are they stationed there to save me from my relatives or from strangers?'

Justice Shankar was by now convinced that all this drama of saluting and guard-change drills were mere formalities, more for show and entertainment than for his family's safety. And he had had enough of it. The poor registrar, unable to perform his duty for no fault of his own, was naturally worried. It was his job to see to the safety and comfort of the judges. Ultimately, he requested the chief justice of the High Court to intervene.

It was decided to have the post removed but guards in plain clothes would be put on duty around Justice Shankar's house round the clock. However, this would be a secret arrangement and Justice Shankar was not to find out about it.

The entire High Court was talking about the ghastly bomb blast at Justice Shankar's residence. They were all concerned about his and his family's safety. In their own small ways, they were praying for the safety of their esteemed Judge Saab and his family. In full faith they gave little talismans to him to drive the enemies and the danger away. One advocate offered prayers in the temple and brought him prasad. Someone gave him special trinkets to wear to ward off evil eyes, someone got a special copper leaf from the Devi's temple with vermilion applied on it to keep in his pocket all the time. There was black thread brought from Kali's temple to tie around his neck; others even performed special puja and recited the Mahamrityunjay jaap for his safety and protection.

Judge Saab was deeply touched by people's gestures and concern. He appreciated their warm feelings and very humbly accepted all their offerings and deposited all the tokens in front of his own deity, in the small temple he had in the north-east corner of his house. One could hear him speaking softly to his deity, 'Thank you, my lord, for all the love and care you have bestowed upon me through my fellow beings! I very humbly place all these tokens at your feet for safe-keeping. I am not scared because I know that you are my saviour, and you are with me all the time. Hari om tatsat.' With this, he finished his prayer and felt stronger for it.

19

It was Dr Sharan's turn to get flummoxed by Kishen Das's reports. Everything was normal, perfectly within range. Then where was the disturbance coming from? Maybe it was psychosomatic! Perhaps some childhood incident could throw some light on the matter. Maybe some birth defect or shock of some kind! Had there been an oxygen shortage at the time of his birth in some of his brain cells? There was no clue that he could gather from the medical reports. Kishen Das, just eighteen years of age, was tall, good-looking and healthy. His thought processes were in perfect order and he led a stress-free life at home. Yes, father and son often fought with each other, but at the same time, they could not do without each other. They cared for each other and bonded well. There was no dearth of love, affection and respect in their relationship. After his mother's death, his father had made sure that he gave him enough love and understanding to compensate for Kishan's loss. The earlier generations were also healthy, so this disorder was not inherited.

Love, they say, heals all kinds of wounds and illnesses— physical as well as mental. Strange though it may sound, Kishen's ailment had become aggravated and more pronounced only after he found his first love, Seema. It seemed quite strange because she was a faithful friend. They were happy together. Then what was it that had brought about the sickness? There were no clear indications. Seema's father was very fond of Kishen. He was well received and respected in Seema's family. There were no objections to their friendship whatsoever. Seema was also good-looking, pleasant and well brought up. There was nothing out of the ordinary that could have upset Kishen. Why then did he get the fits?

It had started with just stiffness in his neck accompanied by shooting pain, but today he had also fainted. Surely he was strong enough to witness the sight of an injured body being wheeled into a hospital! What had actually upset him? What unusual thing did he see in that unknown guard?

The doctor tried as hard as he could, but was unable to find the smallest clue to solve the mystery. This was indeed a complicated case. Dr Sharan had visited Kishen's home, met his father and other relatives. Now he was going to meet Seema and her family. Kishen was driving him to Seema's residence at Pataliputra, a posh colony of Patna.

On the way to Seema's house, Dr Sharan opened the conversation with Kishen, 'Since when have you known this girl?'

'Since eternity,' Kishen smiled. 'Seema is her name.'

'Seema, okay, and have you known her family also since eternity?'

Kishen laughed. 'No, no, they came into my life much later.'

Dr Sharan found Kishen a very interesting person. 'Oh! I see. And do you like them?'

'Oh yes! Her father is such a gem! Not at all like my father.'

'Why? What is wrong with your father?'

'His IAS mania. Otherwise, he is the best father I could have asked for!'

'I see. So he did not get you, you asked for him?'

Kishen was a little embarrassed. 'Doctor Uncle, times have changed, you know?'

Dr Sharan liked Kishen's spontaneity and sense of humour.

Kishen told Dr Sharan that when he had met Seema's father for the first time, her father used to be an ardent follower of Daataa Anand. But he had left the organization since then. Kishen looked a little lost for a while and then, as if he suddenly remembered something, he continued his narration. 'He was full of Daataa Anand and his spirituality, but I never took interest in such subjects, so I did not even pay attention to all that he said. But I kept nodding— had to impress the girl's father you see!' Dr Sharan smiled.

However, Kishen disclosed that when he returned home after his first encounter with his would -be in-laws, he started feeling a bit restless. His head became heavy—it may have been the heat, it was unbearably hot that day—and it was on that night that he had the attack for the first time. He did not know what had happened, but his father told him later that he had started screaming in a very strange voice and they could not decipher the words that he was uttering.

Dr Sharan did not find any connection between Seema's father talking about his guru and Kishen falling sick the same night. It was more likely that the heat had taken its toll. There was nothing alarming in this conversation and in any case, Kishen had mentioned that he had switched off and had not listened to the stories of Daataa Anand as he found that topic quite boring.

Dr Sharan did not think that he needed to analyse Seema's father's spiritual journey with Daataa Anand. But he felt that if Kishen had his first attack after meeting him, then there had to be something more to it. Could the father have tried to impress upon Kishen that they were superior in some way? That he did not measure up to his expectations? Did he, in some way, make him feel small? Did the meeting bring about a split personality in Kishen to the surface? There was nothing new to this chain of thought. Such things happen. It was quite possible. Many a father is unable to accept the fact that his little doll has found a man for herself and he has had no role to play in her choice.

However, after meeting Seema and her family, Dr Sharan cleared his mind of all these doubts. They were more than willing to help the doctor and they adored Kishen. No, it had to be something else.

They talked about various things, sipping tea with typical Bihari evening snacks: nimki, halwa and pakodas with dhania chutney. They discussed Daataa Anand and the criminal case, the bomb blast at Justice Shankar's residence. Nobody noticed that while they talked about the case, Kishen had his gaze fixed at one point on the floor. He just sat there, rigid and stiff; seemingly unconcerned, reticent, lost in his own thoughts, as if he was just not there.

Seema saw him and thought he was getting very bored. She pulled him out to their beautiful garden, the lush green lawn sprinkled with colourful blooms all around and exuding an aura of joy and contentment. Kishen appeared relieved when he came out and looked at Seema.

'What happened? You were looking like a blank TV screen in there,' Seema inquired with concern.

'Naturally, you made me sit with the oldies and disappeared, so I switched off,' Kishen responded.

'But they were discussing subjects of your interest, I thought . . .' Then, all at once, she remembered her promises of not broaching topics related to Daataa Anand. She quickly changed the discussion. 'Anyway, good that you came out, I was missing you out here.'

Kishen looked at her and smiled. But Seema felt as if it was a forced smile. As if he was still not quite there. What could be bothering him? How she wished to kiss away all his worries and make him the happiest person on earth. She sincerely hoped that Dr Sharan would be able to pull Kishen out of his misery.

Everything was normal on the way back. Dr Sharan found the patient and the case even more interesting now that he could not find any lead to the disease. Diagnosis was playing hide and seek with him. Physically, the patient was more than fit, while mentally, all appeared to be normal, with no stress, no tension—where then was the catch?

Kishen emphatically denied any negative thoughts hovering in his mind. He had no enemies and was a friendly person, then where and what entangled his unconscious mind? What was binding him so painfully? Something was definitely not correctly wired which played havoc within his mind. But unless there was some indication, how did one treat him? On what basis? With what medicine? Dr Sharan felt he needed to know and understand Kishen a little more to find answers.

Kishen was fine till he was with Dr Sharan. The moment he dropped the doctor at his Fraser Road residence and turned towards his home, he started feeling dizzy. His head became heavy, his eyes were burning and he felt as if someone had clasped a hand around his neck. He controlled his breath and somehow managed to reach home. Heading straight to his room, he fell flat on his cot. At around 4 a.m., Kishen had those nightmares again. He did not see anyone, just heard weird, barbaric laughter, at a distance initially, but coming closer to him with a lightning speed. When the torturous sound engulfed him, he became hysterical, got up from his bed and started running round and round his bed crying, 'Ammmmaaaa . . . Ammmmaaaa . . .' After some time, he fell down, his neck became stiff and he felt as if a sharp needle had been poked in his neck as the familiar excruciating pain seized him.

The next morning, when Dr Sharan heard the details, he noted that the trigger for the fit had to be at Seema's house. At the same time, he also accepted the fact that allopathy had limited options. It did not have the medicines or even a method to treat patients like Kishen. At the most he could give him sedatives, which would provide only temporary relief but not cure him. They would have to find some alternative therapy to treat him. What? Where? How? He did not know.

Dr Sharan was trying to think of other ways to help Kishen Das. Suddenly, he remembered that he had met a visitor of one of his patients some time late the previous year. He had mentioned a Dr Narayanan in Hyderabad who treated unusual cases. He also said that all those patients who had not been able to recover, even after trying various forms of treatment had gone to him and he had been able to cure many of them.

The next day, Dr Sharan had the old files dug out. He found the name and address of the doctor and gave it to Kishen Das. Kishen and his father left for Hyderabad within a week. They managed to trace the doctor and take the earliest appointment possible as they were absolutely desperate for a cure. However, just a day prior to their departure, Kishen attended the court again.

20

Daataa Anand's case seemed very clearcut when it was admitted in the High Court. It was absolutely transparent. Daataa had been caught red-handed from the scene of the crime and all the testimonies indicated clearly that he was the culprit. But even a simple case can become complicated when able lawyers start twisting each and every word to their client's advantage. Playing with language, even taking the help of shameless white lies, was easy for them! Every argument would be going against the culprit in one session, one would think that Daataa Anand was now tightly cornered from all the sides, but in the very next session, he would break all the shackles and come out clean.

There were rumours circulating that the police inspector who had caught him had got a new passport made under some fictitious name and had migrated to some foreign country along with his family. There was a warrant issued in his name when he failed to turn up at the court, but it was of no use. He was not traceable.

The case got unnecessarily prolonged. Eyewitnesses came in, gave firm testimonies, and at the next hearing reversed their statements. It gradually became apparent that Daataa Anand was winning the case. He managed to prove himself to be innocent and to have been maliciously and falsely implicated. The counsel for defence maintained that Daataa's disciples had committed suicide to free themselves of their own personal problems and that Daataa had no hand in it. The public prosecutor failed to contradict these arguments. He had no concrete evidence to prove to the court that this was not true.

Justice Shankar made one last attempt to find the truth. He prodded the prosecution. 'Where is the diary of Anurag Chowdhury alias Daataa Anand which, according to your earlier arguments, the police had recovered from Anurag Chowdhury's bedroom?'

'Actually it did not contain any worthwhile information, my lord, and since I did not want to waste the valuable time of the court, I did not bring it up!' replied the public prosecutor, seeming rather unconcerned.

The judge looked at some notes in his file and pointed out, 'Your words, and I quote: "The diary is one evidence which cannot change its contents, the colour of the ink and the handwriting." Unquote. You had mentioned earlier that Daataa had written in that diary about some experiment he was conducting to conquer death. That he wanted to resurrect the dead, the evidence of which can be found in the diary?'

The public prosecutor smiled nervously, looked at Daataa Anand and said, 'Yes, my lord! But those were just the details of some dreams that he had had that night. Later, I read it again and realized my mistake.'

'I see! And you also talked about him writing that he had dreamed that Kali Ma had blessed him with supernatural powers. You said he mentioned that goddess Kali wanted a few sacrifices at her altar to make him omnipotent?'

Kishen, sitting on one of the back benches, was happy at this new turn of events in the case. The prosecution had perhaps forgotten about this evidence. It was good that Justice Shankar had reminded them.

'Can we have a look at the diary, please?' the judge demanded.

'It has not been submitted, my lord!' the court clerk responded loudly, shuffling his papers.

The public prosecutor found Daataa's eyes glaring at him. He started stuttering and fumbling. He picked up a glass of water from his table, drank it in one gulp and said, 'My lord! I had put . . . kept the . . . I mean that diary in the lock-up, b . . . b . . . but somehow . . . I . . . I found the lock brrra... oken and the diary m . . . missing.' He looked sheepishly at Daataa.

'Oh no! He is a liar. He is a big-time liar!' Kishen said to himself.

The judge burst out at this, 'How could you be so irresponsible? You knew that this was an important document. You had promised to hand it over to the court the next day, and your failing to do so amounts to contempt of court. You could be severely punished for this!' The public prosecutor was in tears.

Justice Shankar felt as if he had failed. Punishing the prosecution would solve nothing. Daataa was deceitfully slipping away from the gallows. The judge had a strong intuition that Daataa was guilty. He was now even more convinced that not just the eyewitnesses, but even the advocates had been heavily dosed with money. It was so obvious! If Daataa was not guilty, then why was he taking such desperate steps, threatening even Justice Shankar in every possible way? Why did the earlier judges suffer the way they did? And where was the inspector who had caught him and knew everything about his misdeeds? Where was Daataa Anand's wife Rachna? Was she alive? Or had they killed her too? And now the diary; why was it stolen? On whose behest did it disappear? These unanswered questions troubled Justice Shankar.

Earlier, too, the judge had tried to cue the public prosecutor in the right direction a number of times, but he was either too dumb or too smart to take those hints. The situation was such that one could not trust anybody even remotely connected with this case. What could a judge do if the lawyers on both the sides were speaking exactly the same language, that of money? Judge Saab was disillusioned and had lost hope.

He seemed to have no proof, no eyewitness, no way of convicting Daataa Anand. He felt helpless. Perhaps for such cases Justice Mukherjee's approach was right, 'Punish them if caught red-handed, without any trial!'

The law that was formed to safeguard the interest of the innocent was now backfiring. It was the culprits who knew all the loopholes and had managed to wriggle out easily. And the innocents were being hammered for their innocence.

Justice Shankar was in a dilemma. He was not getting any significant, concrete reason to sentence Daataa Anand. When he viewed the situation in its entirety, he realized that if he let him go free, his own conscience would be troubled. Besides, he would be crushing the hope that the general public had reposed in him. They had infinite faith in his fair and fearless judgement and that would be questioned! People would think, and say, that Judge Saab was scared of the threats he was getting! Or even worse, his integrity would be questioned. 'Bribes dictated the judgement,' would be the people's verdict. His hard-earned, well-deserved reputation was at stake, and this fact was worse than a nightmare for him.

On the other hand, however, Justice Shankar's hands were tied. He had to stay within the legal framework and quote legal points, references and precedents for the conclusions he had reached when dictating the sentence. How he wished that he was a police officer! He felt that they had all the power. Had he been one, today Daataa Anand would not have the guts to look up and smile at the judge's helplessness.

Immersed in his dilemma, Justice Shankar sat feeling low and defeated. Suddenly, the shrill tone of his telephone shook him out of his reverie. He picked it up. Slowly, an expression of shock and disbelief spread across his face as he listened intently.

It was a woman's voice. Speaking as if she was in a great hurry, she said, 'Daataa Anand's wife Rachna wants to meet you. She said she will come to the court and give all the evidence required to nail Daataa. But please reserve the judgement till she meets you in the court.' The words rushed out in a desperate hurry. By the time Justice Shankar had recovered enough to ask about the mysterious caller's identity, she had disconnected.

21

Justice Shankar was shaken. He desperately wanted more information but the lady had disconnected. Could she really be calling up on behalf of Daataa Anand's wife Rachna? Why hadn't she told him the whole thing? What exactly was it that Rachna wanted to tell him? Did she really have some concrete evidence? When would she come? Where was she?

Besides, the hearing of the case was almost over. Justice Shankar could not keep the judgement pending for very long. He remembered that he had earlier requested the telephone department to tap his telephone because of the crank calls that he was getting those days. Should he have this call traced by them? But he rejected this idea as soon as he thought of it. It could be dangerous for Rachna. What if Daataa Anand came to know that she had called up? He would leave no stone unturned to find and kill her. That she had managed to survive for so long was by itself a miracle.

Judge Saab was finding his life becoming complicated at every step. His body felt drained and the spirit to fight was ebbing. Was it age catching up or mental exhaustion? The primary emotion that kept running through his head was one of incredulity. How was it that people lacked the confidence and the nerve to tell the truth? He was extremely pained to see the state of affairs in society. To Justice Shankar it felt as if it had been easier to fight the British. The war of independence had been a war of principle. People had the moral courage and strength to face the consequences of their actions. But now the moral fabric of society was badly tattered. No one cared for what was right and what was wrong. Self-interest was all that mattered.

Just then, a peon came and informed Justice Shankar that some journalists wanted to meet him. A day before, the parliament had been dissolved and Madam Gandhi had announced elections. The journalists wanted to know what Judge Saab had to say on the issue. He did not want to say anything about the turn of events. He simply did not want to get involved with the journalists, but it was not that easy to avoid them. They had managed to barge into his chamber.

'Sir, you have been bold enough to defy Madam whenever you thought that she was wrong. Do you think she is right now to have called for elections?'

'Why don't you ask the common people? They are the majority, their views should count, not mine,' said the judge.

'The public wants to hear you, sir, on this issue,' one journalist said.

Justice Shankar had to give in. 'She should have

announced elections the day she lost the Allahabad court case. Had she resigned that day, she would have won the heart, the love and respect of millions, including me, overnight. However, it is we who put dictators on a pedestal and it is we who are crushed underfoot. Spinelessly, we accept their wrongdoings and illegal orders. Licking their boots for small personal gains! Anyway, better late than never. It is good that she has woken up. Whatever be the reason for announcing elections now, I welcome her decision.'

Then the journalists turned to the Daataa Anand case.

'Sir, what is going to be Daataa Anand's fate?'

The judge refused to comment.

They kept pestering him with more questions, 'Sir, do you think that the allegations were true and the witnesses are being bought over?'

The judge did not reply.

And then, most unexpectedly, they dropped a bombshell. 'Do you think Daataa Anand's wife Rachna is alive and absconding? Will she appear at the eleventh hour to give her testimony?'

Judge Saab was absolutely stunned. He was not prepared for such a question, but he managed to hide his reaction. 'If she does, then you will learn about it in course of time,' he replied politely. His heart was racing at the suddenness of the question.

'Did she say that to you?' Being inquisitive is a journalist's bread and butter; they persisted relentlessly.

The questions were now crossing limits so Justice Shankar simply folded his hands and asked the journalists to leave.

He said, 'You will get all your answers after the judgement is delivered in the court. Please excuse me till then and thank you very much.'

After they left, the judge sat, perplexed. How was it that these journalists had suddenly thought of Rachna? Were they such adept sleuths with vast networks of information that they could have found out that someone had rung him up and talked about Rachna? He did not have an answer to any of the questions, but if the case took the turn that it was then promising to take, there might still be a ray of hope. It had been an exhausting day for the judge and he was happy to be finished with it.

22

Dr Narayanan's clinic was in an old house in Himayat Nagar, Hyderabad. He lived there too, and had turned two large rooms into his workplace. The house had been painted perhaps just once—the year it was built in. It looked ancient and distinctly like a decaying monument—age-weary surroundings, walls made green by fungus. There was a jungle-like garden too, with more weeds than plants or flowers.

Of the two rooms inside, one was his office where he welcomed his patients with a peculiar toothy grin. The other was a large, round room where he experimented with his technique, practising it on every new patient. This room had a well-cushioned, comfortable couch in the centre. Surprisingly, unlike the exterior of the house, the interior was neat and well kept.

The walls were a deep salmon pink, the ceiling navy blue

with small recessed blue bulbs, twinkling like stars in the sky. The overall décor was strange. It transported the patients to some other world. Perhaps the set up was to match the doctor's modus operandi.

Dr Narayanan himself looked quite outlandish and unearthly. Thick, long, silvery hair, brown eyes, much too large for his face, and lips like two thin lines drawn with a pointed pencil. And the chin seemed missing. His serpentine beard was divided into two parts and hung straight from below the ears. His clothes were also rather original and matched his personality. A flowing robe, which had lost its sheen and looked more dull grey than black, hung down to the knees and a purple sash was tied around his paunch. He wore a white pyjama underneath.

People who came to him often wondered if he had ever seen his own reflection in a mirror! They were sure he would have fainted had he ever done that. He looked ghastly. However, when coupled with his reputation as a doctor who could tame the most stubborn illness, his persona only lent a mysterious aura to the doctor rather than making him appear ridiculous.

Very soon, one afternoon, Kishen found himself lying on the couch in Dr Naraynan's clinic, trying to figure out a solution to his peculiar problem. It was blissfully quiet in the room. The light was dim and the fragrance of fresh flowers pervaded.

Dr Narayanan had a very soft, velvety voice. He started by telling Kishen that his line of treatment was so different that a lot of people took it as a joke. And those who came just to test the doctor's skill and to make fun of him would not benefit from it. Cure was a fifty-fifty effort by both the doctor and the patient. It was only when the patient cooperated fully that his treatment would work. So if Kishen was ready to give his full support, he would be able to start, otherwise all efforts were futile. Kishen was actually quite nervous and skeptical. He was not at all sure what was expected of him. Nevertheless, he was ready and willing to do whatever was required of him. He told the doctor so. The doctor asked Kishen matter-of-factly if he believed in rebirth!

'Rebirth?' Kishen found this question odd. It also made him a little weary. What had rebirth got to do with his illness? Oh dear! This was another wild goose chase. They had undertaken such a long, tedious journey, spent so much energy and effort, and all of it was to go down the drain!

Then he resolved to think positively about the situation. Since they could not recover the money, time and energy spent, why not learn something about rebirth and then get back to Patna to Daataa Anand's case?

He replied to the doctor that he had heard about rebirth, but knew nothing about it.

Dr Naraynan started explaining that when a person dies his body decays, but the incidents of his life are clearly etched on his mind and stay there. The soul travels out of the body, invisibly carrying this mind along. He tried to elaborate further, 'Sometimes we put things in storage and forget about them! Then, in the course of time, some of these items rot and stink. The foul smell makes us feel sick. So, we hunt for the rotten object, don't we?'

Kishen agreed.

'And when we find the decayed stuff, we throw it away, clean up the store, and everything goes back to normal, right?' the doctor asked.

'Yes,' Kishen nodded.

'Likewise, our mind is a store, stuffed with memories of our past lives, and these memories are dormant. And from this store, sometimes, an unpleasant, unhappy memory begins to leak in minuscule proportions. What triggers it is something that we are unable to understand, but they play havoc with our lives. The day we find out what it is, it will stop bothering us. You get my point?'

'Yes.'

'Okay. Now my job is just to show a torch to my friends like you. The search operation has to be conducted by you. Just follow the light of the torch, is that clear?'

Clear? Nothing could be more hazy or opaque than this, thought Kishen. He was convinced that he had knocked the wrong door. How the hell was he to recall his past life? He was just an ordinary human being! Yogis, if they tried, could perhaps achieve such a feat, not him? No way. Not possible.

He did not remember half the things of this birth and the therapist wanted him to remember what he did in his past life! Sorry doc, he thought to himself, we are wasting each other's time.

The doctor, used to such reactions, seemed to have guessed Kishen's thoughts and his reluctance to try. He said, 'Well, it is up to you. If you don't want to help yourself in finding the problem, then it is entirely your wish. But one thing you must always remember: when you surrender and give up without trying, then you lose all the opportunities to win over your ailment.'

This observation appealed to Kishen, and he found himself agreeing to try.

The doctor explained that he was going to hypnotize Kishen. He would put him to a deep slumber and help him travel back in time.

'What if I get stuck there?' Kishen asked urgently.

'Don't worry, I'll help you come out.'

Kishen wondered if the doctor was taking some kind of revenge. He felt as if he was trapped. But he had no alternative. He had to follow orders.

And after this vague, preliminary, warm-up round with the doctor, the actual game began. The process itself was quite lengthy. It didn't happen in a day. They had to do a number of sittings to pull the right chords to open a tightly shut door to his past.

Dr Narayanan commenced his operation by dimming the lights. He played records of some extremely soft, soothing music, and asked Kishen to close his eyes. The therapist put his hands very gently on his forehead, running his fingers lightly through his hair. Kishen felt relaxed, and soon became sleepy. The doctor then asked him to count in reverse order from hundred. And every time he clicked his fingers, Kishen should count back one number, stop, and then start counting backwards again.

He explained, 'Say if you are counting ninety-nine, ninety-eight, ninety-seven, and I snap my fingers, then you go back to ninety-eight again and then count down from

ninety-seven, ninety-six, ninety-five, finger click, back to
ninety-six, ninety-five, like that. Keep counting, but don't
forget to go back one number when I snap my fingers.'

Kishen found this interesting. He had not slept well
anyway and this was just the perfect atmosphere for him to
let loose, relax and sleep.

The counting began. By the count of sixty-five, Kishen
was dozing off, his voice was faltering. The doctor whispered
softly in his ears, 'Imagine that you are standing on top of
a staircase, then you start climbing down; slowly, carefully.
When I snap my fingers, climb up one step and then climb
down again.'

Kishen started climbing down. The doctor went up to
a corner table and softly thumped his hands on it. Then
he very quietly tiptoed up to Kishen and asked, 'Did you
hear something?'

Kishen was half asleep. He mumbled, 'Someone is
knocking at the front door, down below.'

'Who is it?' the doctor asked and mimicked the sound of
the door opening.

'It's a man,' Kishen said.

'Is he a relative or a friend?'

'I've never seen him earlier.'

'What does he look like?'

'Weird, scary.'

'Describe him.'

'On his face . . . there is . . . only . . . one eye and one
crooked, hooked nose . . . no lips . . . no mouth, no hair . . .

and . . . and . . . he has one ear on his skull.'

'Would you like to speak with him?'

Kishen said, barely audibly, 'I am scared.'

The doctor picked up a thread, brushed it through Kishen's hands, and said, 'Take this thread and tie him up. First tie his hands, but don't look at him, just keep binding from top to toe.'

There was slight movement in Kishen's hands.

After some time, when Kishen was about to fall asleep, the doctor spoke again, 'Just push him out and shut the door. Come back and sit here on the sofa.'

Kishen was breathing heavily earlier, but as he sat on the sofa in his imagination, things started going back to normal. His eyes were closed and when he relaxed utterly, the doctor knocked on his table again. Kishen's eyeballs began to move.

This time, when he opened the door, a ball of very bright but soothing, glittering, light flashed on his eyes. Kishen blinked and said, 'There is a big ball of white light outside, beckoning me.'

The doctor asked, 'Does it make you feel good?'

'Yes.'

'This is your guardian angel. It will help you find your way. Hold it in your arms,' the doctor spoke soothingly.

Kishen was smiling.

The doctor said, 'Now look up at the sky. Clouds are carrying you. This eternal light, this fairy is taking you back to your past life. How does it feel?'

'I am dizzy, going too fast . . .'

'What do you see?'

'The sky. It is revolving,' Kishen answered.

'Let it turn—it is taking you back to your past life. Now pause for a while. Where are you?' the doctor enquired.

In a very feeble voice, Kishen said, 'Chicago, America.'

The doctor was now excited—he was achieving results, 'What year is this?'

Kishen Das could see a number flash on the sky. He just read it out one by one, 'One . . . eight . . . nine . . . three.'

'Eighteen ninety-three. Okay, can you see which birth of yours is this?'

Again, numbers appeared on the sky, 'One . . . five . . .'

'Oh well, this is your fifteenth birth in human form, good!'

Kishen continued, 'A big cottage . . .'

'Whose cottage is it?'

'I don't know . . . perhaps mine . . .'

'Who else is there with you?'

'Mother.'

'How old are you?'

'Ten.'

'Who else is there in your family?'

'No one. Someone is coming!' Kishen whispered.

'Who?'

'A man in saffron robes, a swami . . . smiling at me . . . a guest at my neighbours'.'

'Do you know this swami?'

'No . . . Mom says . . . he is . . . swami . . . Vivekanand . . . India . . . will give discourse this evening . . .'

'Will you go to hear him speak?'

Kishen was quiet for a while as if he was tired. Then his eyeballs moved again, 'Very crowded . . . swamiji . . . speaking.'

'What is he saying?'

'My brothers . . . sisters . . .' Kishen was smiling, then spoke again in the same incoherent voice, 'I want to go . . . India . . . I want to go . . .'

Dr Narayanan called Kishen's name, gradually turned up the intensity of the lights and patted Kishen on his shoulders.

Kishen opened his eyes. His limbs were stiff. He felt as if he had just returned from a long journey. He was tired. But meeting the swami had been a happy experience.

Dr Naraynan did not want to overdo things on the first day of therapy. He said, 'That is all for today; we will have to do one more sitting tomorrow.'

The whole experience was bizarre and extraordinary for Kishen Das. But he was now ready to cooperate fully with the doctor. He now understood what the therapist had meant when he said that all that Kishen had to do was to follow the light he flashed as a guide. But, at the same time, he also felt that everything that was happening had a surreal quality to it. Could it all be the sheer imagination of a fertile mind, or had he really peeped into his past life? Whatever it was, he was fascinated and was now looking forward to the next trip into the past.

23

Kishen Das and his father were sitting on a bench facing the Tank Bundh. They were admiring the beautiful Hussain Sagar lake that is in the centre of Hyderabad. This bundh connects the twin cities of Secunderabad and Hyderabad and it is a lovely, breezy evening spot.

Kishen had found his therapeutic experience quite fascinating, and he was looking forward to his next session with the doctor, but he was a bit apprehensive too. Was there any truth in the Regressive Hypnosis Therapy—the name Dr Naraynan had described his line of treatment with—that was being applied on him? How could anyone travel back in time or life? No, it was not possible. But then, at the same time, whatever he had seen seemed so very real. He had clearly seen the auditorium. He had clearly heard Vivekanand's speech. How did that happen? He must have gone back in time; he convinced himself that it was all true and so it was

136

better to be positive and expunge the doubts arising in his mind. Thus assuring himself, Kishen felt relaxed and ready, indeed, much more eager to go through the next session now and gain some more knowledge and experience.

His father, on the other hand, was simply amazed. How had it happened? He asked his son if he had read or heard about Swami Vivekanand?

Kishen laughed. 'What are you saying, Pop! Who does not know about Swami Vivekanand? But my knowledge of the great man is strictly common knowledge. I know that he was a great spiritual soul, a social reformer, and a very learned, knowledgeable person. Nothing beyond that. Why do you ask?'

'I was just wondering if your knowledge about the saint was speaking up when you were on the therapist's couch.'

'I wish I *had* read more about him! He seems like an interesting person.'

Kishen's father was puzzled. If Kishen did not know much about him, then how had he connected the year 1893, Chicago and Swami Vivekanand? As far as he knew, it was in 1893 that Chicago had hosted the massive World's Parliament of Religions. Swami Vivekanand was not an invited speaker but he had gone anyway, on the special invitation of a spiritual lady, Mrs George W. Hale. This lady had heard him speak earlier and was so captivated by his pious thoughts and philosophy that she wanted to present him to the world. There could not be a better podium, so she took the liberty of introducing him in the conference. And yes, he was also her house guest. Perhaps, in that life,

Kishen had lived next door, and had had the privilege of meeting the great saint! Earlier, when he landed in Boston, Vivekanand had come in contact with Professor John Henry Wright of Harvard University. After inviting Vivekanand to speak at Harvard and on hearing him say that he did not have the credentials to speak at the Parliament, Wright is quoted as having said, 'To ask for your credentials is like asking the sun to state its right to shine in the heavens.' Wright then addressed a letter to the chairman in charge of the delegates, writing, 'Here is a man who is more learned than all of our professors put together.'

The moment Swami Vivekanand had addressed the large gathering with, 'Sisters and brothers of America!' thunderous applause had greeted him which had lasted nearly two minutes.

Mr Das clearly remembered some portions of that wonderful speech, especially how Vivekanand had deplored radicals. 'Sectarianism, bigotry, and its horrible descendant, fanaticism, have long possessed this beautiful earth. They have filled the earth with violence, drenched it often with human blood, destroyed civilization and sent whole nations to despair. Had it not been for these horrible demons, human society would be far more advanced than it is now.'

So true, pondered Mr Das. He had read Swami Vivekanand's enlightened speech so many times that it was deeply imprinted on his mind. He also recalled the concluding part, which was wonderfully forceful.

'The seed is put in the ground, and earth and air and

water are placed around it. Does the seed become the earth, or the air, or the water? No. It becomes a plant. It develops after the law of its own growth, assimilates the air, the earth, and the water, converts them into plant substance, and grows into a plant.

'Similar is the case with religion. The Christian is not to become a Hindu or a Buddhist, nor a Hindu or a Buddhist to become a Christian. But each must assimilate the spirit of the other and yet preserve his individuality and grow according to his own law of growth.

'If the Parliament of Religions has shown anything to the world, it is this: It has proved to the world that holiness, purity and charity are not the exclusive possessions of any church in the world, and that every system has produced men and women of the most exalted character. In the face of this evidence, if anybody dreams of the exclusive survival of his own religion and the destruction of the others, I pity him from the bottom of my heart, and point out to him that upon the banner of every religion will soon be written in spite of resistance: "Help and not fight," "Assimilation and not destruction," "Harmony and peace and not dissension."'

So relevant, thought Mr Das, and even more so in the present.

India and its religions, its faiths, its multiple ways of life, the deep-rooted feelings, emotions, relationships, the rich Indian culture and its heritage, all got recognition in the speech and Swami Vivekanand established for the first time a towering spiritual identity of India in the Western world.

And after listening to him spellbound, there were many

in the audience who expressed a desire to know India more, and from closer quarters. They received an open invitation to sample Indian hospitality. Perhaps Kishen, in the life he was living in 1893, was also among those invited. But how strange that such a vast, amazing experience could be relived by Kishen in a matter of minutes, thanks to Dr Narayanan's therapy. The more Mr Das thought about it, the more it puzzled him; everything seemed entangled in mystery. On the one hand was science, ever ready to negate thoughts that could not be proven empirically. But on the other, there were these strange experiences, like the one Kishen had, which could neither be explained nor denied? And how could one doubt the evidence of one's eyes? And these questions notwithstanding, Mr Das was desperate to find exactly what it was in his son's past life that was troubling him so much. He earnestly wished and prayed that Dr Narayanan would succeeded in doing whatever it was that he was trying. He could not bear to see his son suffering the way he was.

24

Justice Shankar had begun dictating the judgement to his typist but he found it difficult to concentrate. He found himself wondering what exactly had been there on Rachna's mind? What was it that she had wanted to tell him? Where was she? Who was the woman who had telephoned? Would she call up again? Would he be able to meet her? It was very likely that the information she had held vital importance that could change the entire complexion of the case! Perhaps the truth would come out. However, it was futile to endlessly wait for her. He had to do his job. If and when she would come, he would see how they could help each other. In case her version sounded reliable and truthful, then perhaps she could be made the key witness in the final arguments.

After a while, Justice Shankar got ready and left at his usual time for the court. About an hour after he had left, two women who looked like ragpickers entered the gates of his residence.

There were no guards at the gate to stop them. The two each had a sack hanging behind their shoulders, with waste paper and some rubbish inside them. This was their morning collection. The plain-clothed watchmen, doing their duty around the house, instantly became alert.

Near the main door of the house, the two women called out, 'Anybody home? Hello, can you hear us?'

Birju came outside and scolded them, 'How dare you come inside? Don't you see this is not just anybody's house? Important people live here.'

Birju would never let go of any opportunity to show off. He was always finding ways to impress upon others that as an attendant in Justice Shankar's house, he had celebrity status.

One of them said, 'We are very thirsty, brother, please give us some water.'

This request melted Birju's heart. He would go out of his way to feed hungry people or give water to the thirsty. Birju firmly believed that this was the highest service to god. A man is closest to god when he takes care of the hungry and the thirsty. And he never missed such an opportunity.

After quenching her thirst, one of them took out a dirty, folded chit, wrapped in her saree corner, tucked in the waistline. She handed it to Birju and requested him to read out the address. She said some lady had called her for a job at this address. He gave the chit back to her. Birju's knowledge of alphabets was zilch, but he had to impress upon them that he knew. Carefully hiding his inability to read, he ordered them out. When they still insisted, he instructed them briskly, in a rather business-like way, to go and ask someone else, as he was too busy and had no time to entertain their queries.

But the women would not budge. They were adamant that Birju should ask someone inside the house to help them. Birju was now losing patience. Just as he started shouting at them to get lost, Meera came out. She had been hearing all this commotion for some time. She calmly took the paper, read out the address, and told them the way to their destination. One of them enquired in whispers from Birju, 'Who is this kind lady?'

Birju told them, 'She is our madam. Judge Saab's wife.'

'Okay. Salaam, memsaab, you are very kind,' they said and turned away.

As they reached the gate, one of them came rushing back to Meera, 'Oh, I left the paper in your hand!' She collected the chit from Meera and quickly pushed a bulky envelope into her hand, whispering, 'Important paper, Madam. Hide it!'

Meera was startled. She did not understand what all this was about, but she followed instructions and neatly hid the envelope in the folds of her sari. She quickly went into her bedroom, shut the door, unfolded the paper and read it. She was stunned. In a long letter, Daataa Anand's complete life-story had been written out.

She hid the note in her almirah, locked it, and went out looking for the women. But they had left by then. Birju told Meera that when the two of them went out, a stranger had stalked them and began questioning them very rudely.

'Then?' Meera asked.

'Then one of them told the man that they had come in for water, showed him the address they were going to, and said that if he wanted to talk to them, he could come at the given address.'

Meera was slightly amused. So, this was Daataa Anand's wife. Quite a bomb, to be honest! She then waited anxiously for her husband to come back.

Justice Shankar came home in the evening. He changed into comfortable clothes and went out to the garden. Meera joined him and told him about the events of the afternoon and the letter. The judge was very anxious to know about the contents of the letter, but they both knew that they had to be extra vigilant. They would have to maintain their routine to avoid suspicion of any kind. Anyone could be keeping tabs on them.

Justice Shankar also knew that a criminal like Daataa Anand would not want to take chances at this juncture. Just on the presumption that things were turning in his favour, he would not relax and be complacent.

It was tea time. Judge Saab and Meera talked about various things: elections, the latest political developments, their daytime activities, and then, like on other evenings, Judge Saab got up and went to the bedroom, carefully opened the wardrobe, put the letter in his pocket and headed for the bathroom. As was his wont, he sometimes found it easier to concentrate there.

Judge Saab,

I have a lot of regard and respect for you. I write this to you with full faith that you will do justice. If anybody comes to know that I have come back, they will hunt me out and kill me. Please do not let Anurag Chowdhury go scot-free. He is vicious and a hard core criminal, a murderer. He got all those people killed who discovered the real him. He wants to become 'god', and in his pursuit, he has sacrificed many of his close aides, burnt them alive, and eliminated those who found out about his criminal activities. Forget others, a pervert who can kill his own twelve-year-old son can kill anyone! He is ruthless, he is wicked. I swear by my son's dead body that every word of what I am saying is true. God only knows how he got so immersed and involved in tantra mantra, black magic, that he is no longer a normal human being!

We had a beautiful house in Chandernagore on the bank of a river. I could see the river flowing from my bedroom windows. At night, after everyone had slept, I often saw him through the window, lighting a fire next to the river. He would then kill some animal, drink its blood, then dance around the fire wearing a garland of bones around his neck, ash on his body, a prominent, deep red vermilion tika across his forehead, and make weird noises.

One night, he quietly took away my son and made him sleep in front of him on the green grass. My son was just two years old then. I got very worried. I panicked and fought with him. He was very convincing in his replies.

'Don't worry, Rani, I was doing puja, seeking the lord's blessings for our son.'

I did not understand him then and thought that he was telling the truth. I was deeply touched by how much he cared for our little one. But after that I started hearing all kinds of things about him. His followers had started disappearing suddenly. How many he sacrificed at the altar, only he knows! He never left a trace.

And then, one day, my son disappeared. I went berserk searching for him, but could not find him. When I asked Anurag, he said that I must forget my son for seven years, as he was training him to become a famous spiritual guru. I was hysterical. I pleaded with him that I wanted my son back. He said, 'Don't be so selfish, your son has a very bright future. One day, he is going to be so famous that he will rule the world. But that demands sacrifice from you.' Which mother would not want a bright future for her offspring? I kept quiet. How was I to know that this was a lie?

Months, years passed. When, after seven years, my son did not return, I was perturbed. Though I was barred from entering Anurag's ashram in town, I could not hold myself back any longer. I had to meet my son. I was missing him too much. I went over to the ashram. Anurag was not there. He had left for Hazaribagh early in the morning. I learnt there that Daataa was going to show a miracle that night in the jungles of Hazaribagh. He would bring back to life a child who had been lying dead for the last seven years. Also, he would kill another one, and give his life back to him after an hour. I quietly came out from there and informed the police. I don't know how Daataa's people found out about my visit to the police station. The same evening, his people came and managed to knock me down unconscious. When I opened my eyes, I was lying in the jungle in a strange place. I saw a strange old woman, looking down questioningly at me. I was in Nepal. I had no passport, no money, and no one with me. May god bless that strange old woman who helped me out. The two of us managed to walk back here with great difficulty.

But sir, I found out that on the night the police nabbed him, Daataa had tricked his disciple Rakesh into surrendering at the altar and set him on fire in front of many of his other close aides. The poor chap did not know that he was being sacrificed. He was made to drink a concoction and knocked out unconscious. Then his body was doused completely with oil before his pyre was lit. His only fault was that he had threatened Daataa that he would inform Daataa's mother about all his misdeeds.

Saab, I shiver at the thought of that wicked man's violent deeds. I don't know how to tell you, it pains me, it wrenches my soul completely. I can't stop crying, but you have to be told. Sir, the child he was going to revive that evening was none other than my own son. My poor innocent child had been lying dead at the feet of my husband's deity, his Kali Ma, for seven years!

Sir, please do not hesitate in convicting Daataa and sentencing him to death. He is not a man, he is a beast! A carnivore! A snake that spits venom. He fools people

with his sweet talk and pours poison into their goblets.
With a lot of hopes pinned on you. Waiting for justice.
Rachna.

Justice Shankar had goosebumps all over his body and
tears in his eyes. Was this man a human being or a demon
in human disguise? Daataa defied all laws of humanity and
seemed completely bereft of human emotions and feelings.
Why, even animals did not kill their offspring the way he had.
And killing his own son! For what? Some futile experiment?
All of Justice Shankar's senses were in turmoil. He was
shocked beyond words—horrified, speechless.

But at the same time, his rational mind took over. He
realized that this letter could do nothing in court. Legal
matters demanded evidence! What was the proof that this
letter had been written by Rachna? How did one establish
the fact that Rachna was Daataa Anand's wife? They had
no certificate or witness to vouch for this truth. Leave alone
Daataa's followers, even his mother did not know about her.
And the police inspector who caught him red-handed was
missing. The others who were present at that ghastly site
had withdrawn or turned hostile, changing their statements
one by one.

If Rachna came to the court and narrated the details, it
might help. But she, too, was not an eyewitness. She just
knew that the dead child was her son, but his body had
also been beyond recognition. Who had killed him? When?
Where? She had no answers.

And that fateful evening, in the jungles, when Daataa

Anand was dancing around the fire, holding the dead body of his son in his arms, Rachna had not been present. Then how would her evidence hold up in court? Justice Shankar had never felt so helpless before. He knew the facts, but the court would not accept them.

Emotionally distressed and mentally disturbed, he sat down in his temple, eyes fixed on his deity, his hands folded. He prayed sincerely with his heart and mind, 'Lord Krishna, I am unable to see my path. Please show me the way. It feels as if you are testing me—please guide me. Please help me! Help me find justice. I beg of you.' There were tears in his eyes.

25

Kishen Das reached Dr Narayanan's clinic at the appointed hour. He was feeling quite confident. After a few sessions, he knew what was expected of him. He was relaxed and determined to try his best and even if nothing came out of the sessions, nothing was lost. He felt relieved and the preliminary exercise had already started giving him peace of mind.

However, it is not so simple to slip back into previous lives, to try to sift out past clutter to straighten the present. And one's imagination does take one places too. Like it took Kishen to Chicago the other day. Who knows, Switzerland could be his next destination! Kishen smiled. He was feeling light and rejuvenated after having had a conversation with Seema over the telephone. He told her about the food he was eating at Hyderabad and how he wished she was sharing it with him. Seema said that she was missing him a lot and wanted him to come back soon. Kishen had wanted to hear exactly that and so he was grinning from ear to ear all as he took his place on Dr Narayanan's couch. Dr Narayanan asked Kishen the reason for his grin.

'My girlfriend Seema has sent you regards, sir!' Kishen replied pleasantly. Dr Narayanan nodded acceptance and patted Kishen affectionately on the head.

And then Dr Narayanan and Kishen went back to their serious business. The routine was the same. The lights were dimmed, Kishen counted backwards, he stepped down the stairs, there was a knock on the door. But this time, the doctor noticed that Kishen was uneasy climbing down the stairs. He would shiver every now and then in his hypnotized state. The doctor asked him if there was any problem. Kishen did not reply, but it was evident that his neck was hurting and becoming stiff. The doctor gently slipped his arms around Kishen's neck for support and softly stroked his eyebrows. Kishen's eyes were half open and he looked drowsy.

He whispered slowly, 'It's him . . . it's him.'

'Who is it?' the doctor enquired, matching Kishen's tone.

'My neck . . .' Kishen began sobbing uncontrollably.

Dr Narayanan held Kishen in his arms and said with affection, 'Nothing will happen to you, son, don't worry. I am there . . . I am with you my child . . . you are not alone!' The doctor brushed Kishen's hair gently with his fingers to reassure him.

When Kishen was a little composed, the doctor lay him down carefully on his couch and closed the patient's eyelids with his palms. Then, for a little while, he just moved his fingers, first in a clockwise and then in an anticlockwise motion, right above Kishen's forehead. After that, the therapist began to whisper in a stern voice, still moving his fingers, 'Today you will be caught. You have given enough trouble to poor innocent people. Today you cannot hide yourself; I can see you clearly. You are there, beneath the open blue sky. I can see a jungle and then a house and there is . . .'

Before the doctor could complete his sentence, Kishen spoke up, 'A river!'

The doctor asked, 'Where is the river?'

'Behind that house,' was Kishen's response.

'Whose house is it?'

'The boy's.'

'How old is the boy?'

'Five years old.'

'Do you know him?'

Kishen was quiet for a while and then said, 'It's me.'

'Which year are you in?' Kishen looked up at a figure in the sky. '1957.'

The doctor was finally getting some answers. 'Where is this house?'

'Chandernagore.'

'Who else is there in that house?'

'Nobody. Ma has gone out.'

'Where has she gone?'

Kishen was mum, and then he quietly said, 'He has come.'

'Who has come?'

Kishen did not say anything.

'Are you going somewhere?'

'He is taking me.'

'Where is he taking you?'

There was no answer from Kishen.

The doctor tried to feel Kishen's breath with his hands close to his nose. Kishen's breathing was becoming uneven, heavy and fast. Kishen was in distress. With a lot of pain and agony in his voice, he said. 'He is twisting my neck. It hurts. He is making me drink something.'

'Who is he?'

'Da . . . da . . . aaaa . . . nd . . . my father.'

'Is he beating you?'

'No. He has opened . . . a small door . . . behind . . . almirah . . . in his room . . . taken me there . . . a closed room from all sides.'

'What else is there in that room?'

'Darkness . . . Kali Ma . . . bones . . . twisted my neck with bones on both sides . . . muzzled me, sprays something on me . . . every day . . .' Kishen was sobbing by now.

'What happened?'

'Too long . . . in this dingy room . . . neck twisted . . . pokes my neck with a needle . . . every day . . . till I bleed . . . puts a tika on his forehead with my blood. It hurts . . . call my mother . . . please . . . call her . . .' And then Kishen began crying and howling, much like a small child would. 'He will kill me tomorrow! He said so to Kali Ma . . . I am scared . . . call my mother . . . Amma . . . please call her . . .'

'What else did he tell Kali Ma?'

'He will kill me tomorrow . . . and then bring me back to life . . . with her help . . .'

'When will he revive you?'

'After seven years . . .'

'Where is your mother?'

'I don't know . . . searching for me.'

'Do you recognize her?'

Kishen was extremely tired by now. He looked mentally, emotionally and physically drained. He was about to drop off to sleep but he managed a whispered answer before dozing off, 'Yes, I recognize my mother.'

The doctor let him sleep. Then he called Kishen's father to his consultation room. 'You can take him home if you wish,' he advised. 'Since Kishen has managed to find the cause of his malady, the treatment is over. You can contact me if the problem persists, but I don't think it will. However, Kishen is likely to sleep for a long time, as it normally happens with my patients after such sessions. They are exhausted and need rest, physical as well as mental. Let him sleep till he gets up on his own. And please do not ask him any questions as he has already gone through a lot of trauma.'

Mr Das had tried hard to listen to Kishen talking but could not decipher his whispers. Only Dr Narayanan could decipher his murmur because he was used to it.

Dr Narayanan told Mr Das everything that Kishen had said about his past life. Mr Das kept shaking his head. He was shocked beyond words—such a horrendous tale! He could not believe it. 'No, Kishen must have been imagining or hallucinating. How could he see his past life? Not possible!' was his first reaction. But then he checked with Dr Narayanan to see if all this could be true. The doctor just nodded his head while making some notes in his diary.

Kishen's father was absolutely puzzled. He said, 'No, then it is not Dada Anand as you mentioned, but there is one Daataa Anand.' Mr Das tried to assimilate the story for a while and then said, 'No wonder! No wonder! I guess that must be the reason for Kishen taking so much interest in Daataa's court case!'

'Who is Daataa Anand?' The doctor had not heard of the name.

Mr Das narrated the Daataa Anand story. Dr Narayanan heard it all with great interest and was aghast and horrified. He advised that Kishen would perhaps remain restless till Daataa was properly punished, but there was nothing to worry about.

The doctor further elaborated, 'Kishen will be free of those attacks now. He will feel much lighter and his neck will not turn and twist like earlier.' He further emphasized that Kishen had released his dormant fears, understood his subconscious mind, found the reason for his pain and discomfort, and realized that all this had happened in his past life. 'Kishen may now try to take revenge on his previous birth father, or else may go out of his way to help the court deliver justice. He may even try to find his mother. If he tries any of these, let him. It will cool down the pent-up fire inside his mind, body and soul. He will then be at peace with himself. However, he will dwell over all this just for a short while. After that, he will come back completely to this life, a much happier and well-adjusted person. You need not worry about him any more,' concluded the doctor.

Mr Das thanked Dr Narayanan profusely. The past few days had been an eye-opener for him, and there was a lot he had to understand. Mr Das managed to put his sleeping son in the taxi with a little help from the doctor's assistant and drove back to the circuit house. He was immensely grateful to the doctor and felt that Dr Narayanan was nothing short of a magician.

And now, Mr Das had become a convert. He had no sympathies for Daataa Anand whatsoever. How could any father be so cruel? How could he torture his own son? Anyone who could twist his son's neck and keep him imprisoned in a black hole had to be mentally deranged! Such a man should be thrown out from society and given the severest punishment possible! Mr Das was livid with anger. He wished he could tell the complete story and get Daataa lynched at the Gandhi Maidan so that no one would ever dare to become like him.

But, back in Patna, Mr Das had to keep quiet about Dr Narayanan's handling of the ailment. He felt that people would not understand or appreciate the unique method of treatment. It could become a joke and Mr Das would rather die than let anyone laugh at his son or him. He was also quite sure that there was no way his story would stand up in court. How would he prove that Kishen was Daataa's son in his previous life? How would he satisfy the court about the phenomenon of rebirth itself? Such limitations! God! Why do you play with human lives and emotions? It is not fair that you show one the road to victory and then lock up the entrance, he thought. How fickle, how empty is the society we live in? And what purpose do laws serve? A liar gets away with murder but when a person telling the truth points his finger at the culprit, he has to substantiate his allegation with evidence; find eyewitnesses, who are easily bought over by the criminals. For criminals like Daataa Anand it is as easy to dodge and fool the court as it is to kill mercilessly.

26

Kishen Das was back in Patna. After the sittings with Dr Narayanan, he found uncanny similarities between his past and present life. In his previous birth, he had lost his mother when he was five years old. In the present too, when his mother died, Kishen had been just five years old. Obviously, he was not fated to have his mother's love and affection for a longer period. In his last birth, his father was a wicked, brutal beast. In this life, though, his father loved and cared for him. But what a terrible Hitler he was at times! Along with these thoughts, the one person who kept coming into his mind was his mother from his previous life: Rachna. Was she still alive? Her name had come up a number of times in the Daataa Anand case, but where had she disappeared since then? Could Daataa Anand have also kept her captive in the same black hole adjacent to his bedroom? But his house was fully searched. The room behind the almirah was also flushed. Nothing was found. Actually, Daataa had got prior information of the impending search and he had had the bones and the image of Kali Ma removed from there well in time.

Where could Rachna be? Tormented by Daataa's brutality, had she broken down? Kishen wondered if he would be able to recognize her if he ever came face to face with her. He remembered fondly how beautiful she had looked in his hypnosis-induced trance! She was tall, with sun-kissed skin, and her thick, long plait swayed gently when she walked. And the red coin-sized bindi which glowed on her forehead, together with the vermilion in her parted hair, made her look even more radiant. He wondered if he would ever be able to meet her. And if he did, would he recognize her? Would she acknowledge him? And if she did, would she run her silky fingers through his hair and say, 'Amaar shonamun, my sweet son?'

And Daataa Anand? What should he be called? A sinner unsurpassed or a butcher? Would he get the death sentence? And what about all the witnesses who had turned hostile. It appeared as if nobody had seen anything. Nobody knew anything. Then how would justice be served? Should he go and meet Justice Shankar and tell him the story of his past life? He might find some clue somewhere to nail the culprit. Yes. That would be the right thing to do. But it was very late at night. Kishen Das made up his mind to go to the judge the next morning. He had heard that it was not difficult to meet Justice Shankar. He was approachable to anybody who went to him with genuine problems. And having made up his mind, Kishen turned over and fell asleep.

The next day, at 7 a.m., he took his father's car without permission and turned it towards Justice Shankar's residence.

27

In those days, Durga Puja was celebrated in Bihar with much gusto and fanfare. Every locality had a pandal, and Ma Durga's idols were placed centrestage. The Patna Durga Puja was also famous for its unique music soirées that ran all night. The best classical artistes from all over India used to consider it an honour to be invited there. The entire town would be up and about the whole night. People travelled from one location to the other, with family and friends, searching for their favourite artistes. Entry was free and yet there used to be complete decorum and order. All around the venue people sat on their rickshaw seats, motorcycles, the roofs of their cars on tree branches, enjoying the music. They moved quickly to the next destination as soon as one performance was over. It was only when Ustad Bismillah Khan softly touched the notes of Raga Bhairavi on his shehnai to usher in the morning that one realized that the night was bowing out to dawn.

Unaware of and unconcerned with the soul-touching music of the maestros, Daataa Anand woke early, got into his car, and drove towards the Patna Airport for his morning walk. It was his daily ritual. His gun-toting guards would follow him up to a point and then sit down at a tea shop and sip tea. Only one guard used to walk six steps behind him all through his walk.

Daataa had no idea that he was being watched every day. He had no inkling that somebody was recording his movements—how far he walked, how efficient his bodyguards were, how smart the person who walked behind him was, how sharp his reflexes were. If someone tried talking to Daataa on his walk, how would he react? A plan was being chalked out after ascertaining all these details.

On Vijaya Dashami, the tenth day of the Durga Puja, Daataa was walking when suddenly, from behind a tree, a ragpicker appeared. She was carrying a dirty bag, which she quickly put down on the ground and bent double to touch Daataa's feet chanting *Anandam hi anandam*. The armed guard hurriedly charged up, caught her and asked her to disappear from there at once. The woman looked straight into Daataa's eyes and said, 'This behaviour with your devotee, Daataa?'

Daataa kept quiet. He did not react.

The woman said that if the guard were to leave them alone, she would to tell him something that concerned a threat to his life. Daataa scrutinized her. She was frail and old, with not much strength left in her body. He guessed she must be sixty years old. She certainly did not look strong enough to harm him. He asked his guard to leave them alone.

Walking with him for a while, the beggar-woman started talking in a mix of Magahi, a Bihari dialect, and broken Hindi. She said, 'Do you know that your wife Rachna is in town and that she has even met Judge Saab? She has assured him that she will go to court and be a witness against you.'

This startled Daataa Anand, and he became wary.

'How do you know all this?' he asked her.

'Daataa, am I a liar? Don't I care for your life?'

'How can you convince me that you are telling the truth?' Daataa asked her.

'Daataa swami, she was loitering around here and there, then I gave her shelter. I did not know her identity.'

'Then how did you find out?'

She continued in her dialect, 'One day, she insisted that she wanted to go to the judge's house. She said that she wanted to find out about somebody's address. She fooled me with this excuse and quietly handed over a chit to Judge Saab's wife. When I asked her about it, she told me that the letter contained a complete account of some convict's crimes, based on which the accused could easily be hanged. I knew that your case was in his court, so I became suspicious.

'That night I checked her bag. It confirmed my doubts. Then I asked her point-blank about her identity. She made me swear that I would not tell anybody, and then she disclosed that she was Rachna. That night itself I made up my mind that I must come and inform you. But such a bitch that woman is—she disappeared the same night. But let me tell you, she is going to reach the High Court with Judge Saab in his car the day after tomorrow when the judgement will be pronounced.'

'Is she hiding in his house?' Daataa asked her.

'No, Daataa, I don't know her whereabouts now, but I know for sure that she will come to the petrol pump diagonally opposite the High Court. Judge Saab will pick her up from there.'

Daataa was now a worried man. Yes, now he remembered. His spies had told him just the other day that two beggar-women had entered Justice Shankar's compound. But they were harmless, as they were merely searching for someone's address. Well now, so one of them was Rachna! And she was alive, and trying to take revenge. Oh I see! he thought grimly.

'How do you know that she will come to the petrol pump? Who told you?' Daataa wanted to make sure before taking action.

'Daataa, if you don't believe me, it is perfectly fine. I am your true devotee and so it was my duty to tell you. Now at least I will not feel guilty that I did not warn you well in advance.' Having said this, she turned to go.

Daataa stopped her. 'Is it possible for me to meet Rachna?'

'Where? I myself am looking for her now because that thief stole my clothes, my ten rupees and ran away. She cheated and fooled a poor woman like me. That greedy bitch took away whatever she could lay her hands on, including some eatables that I had stored!'

'Can you recognize her?' Daataa enquired.

'Of course! That filthy woman, scratching herself with her dirty black nails, her hair full of lice, that tall witch—why will I not recognize her?'

'Okay, so then you will come with me that day?' Daataa asked.

'Which day?'

'The day of the judgement?'

'Why? Why should I come with you?' the old woman wanted to know.

'We will reach the petrol pump before Justice Shankar arrives and kidnap Rachna.'

'No, Daataa, I will not come with you.'

'Why?'

'Because you move around with twenty gunmen protecting you. Suppose Rachna runs away and they open fire and the bullets hit me instead, making holes in my body all over, then? I don't even have money for treatment. No, no. I am scared of such a situation. She is your wife. You will have to manage her by yourself. If you want to make fun of your marriage in front of your bodyguards, then it is your wish. I will not be a part of all this. Please let me go.'

Daataa said, 'No, nobody will be there with me. I will tackle Rachna myself. But you will have to come with me. Not just come, you will have to make Rachna agree, at all costs, to come to the car in which I will be waiting. The rest, I will manage. And yes, you will be rewarded handsomely for this favour.'

The woman stood thinking for a while and then said, 'Okay, I can even lay down my life in your service. Whatever happens will happen. Even if I die, it will be for you, my lord! It is all right. So tell me when I should come to the petrol pump. I don't have a watch, but that does not matter, I will ask someone.'

Daataa Anand speculated on all the pros and cons of the plan for a while and then decided that he did not want to take any chances. Suppose the woman did not turn up. She did not have a watch either. She could get delayed.

He emphasized, 'You will come with me right now. Stay in the ashram and from there we will go together to our destination.'

'No, my lord! I am too small a person to live in your ashram, amongst your esteemed guests. Honestly, such a desire has never crossed my mind, not even in my wildest dreams. Please excuse me!' The ragpicker folded her hands in respect to Daataa, picked up her soiled sack from the road and turned around to go.

Daataa Anand was stumped by the old woman's revelations. And there was no way he could let her go and, consequently, invite trouble for himself. What if she did not turn up? He was absolutely convinced that the woman had genuine concern for him. He did not want to let matters slip out of his hands. He caught hold of the woman's arm and called her 'Ma'. And then, showing respect, he spoke up in a theatrical manner, 'Whenever a child is in trouble, it is always the mother who comes forward to protect him. You are also like my mother. If you don't help me, then who will?

Don't worry about my foreign guests—they don't believe in caste and creed, rich or poor, they have such great humility in them that they welcome and accept everyone equally with open arms. You must not feel inferior to them in any way, Ma, after all, I am with you! Yes, only one request, please do not talk about these things with anyone in the ashram or outside.'

The ragpicker looked as if she had not anticipated such a reaction. She seemed confused for a while. But when she saw that Daataa was firm and would not let her go at any cost, she seemed to decide these was no option. Perhaps she thought that she would be better off in the ashram with two square sumptuous meals and a better place to sleep in. She put her sack carefully in the dickey of the car and sat with Daataa on the rear seat.

28

Kishen Das reached Justice Shankar's residence early in the morning. Judge Saab was having his morning tea along with his family members. This was family time, and the morning tea was accompanied by spicy election gossip. Mrs Gandhi's diminishing popularity and the Congress's disdainful attitude during the Emergency was being scrutinized.

Justice Shankar was unusually quiet, pensive and aloof, as if he was lost in a dark and dreadful jungle, thorny shrubs and intermingled branches blocking his every step. It was like there was no way out for him. Meera asked him if he was feeling well.

He reflected, 'People think that a convict's fate is in the hands of a judge. I wish it really was true. But unfortunately, our legal systems weave such a web around a judge's jurisdiction that he can do nothing.'

Before Meera could ask him the reason for his statement,

Birju came and informed them that a gentleman had come to meet Judge Saab.

'Who is he? What has he come for?' Meera asked.

'He says he will tell every thing to Judge Saab.'

Meera was alarmed. She indicated to Birju that he was to accompany the judge.

Judge Saab thought the stranger looked somewhat familiar. Kishen Das introduced himself. He told Justice Shankar that he had been attending his court regularly, sitting on the last benches. Justice Shankar smiled and nodded. He asked Kishen to sit down and enquired about the purpose of his visit.

Birju, who was still standing at the door, understood that the situation was safe. He asked if the guest would have something to drink and then left them alone.

Kishen disclosed that he had been ringing up Judge Saab's residence as a 'well-wisher' and had promised to present himself at an appropriate time.

'Oh, I see! So that was you. Hmm, any particular reason why I should worry about threats to my life?' The judge asked without beating about the bush.

This was exactly what Kishen had come to tell him. He said that earlier he had no idea why he was taking such a keen interest in the case, and why he was so worried about Judge Saab's safety, but now he had all the answers. And then Kishen narrated how he used to suffer from a mysterious disease, and how Judge Saab's nephew Dr Sharan had sent him to Hyderabad, and what had happened in Dr Narayanan's clinic. His journey into his past life, and all that he had discovered about Daataa Anand. How his father had tortured and killed him. How he wanted to experiment and test his spiritually acquired power on his son. What a cruel man he was. He was a murderer, all allegations against him were true and he must be hanged.

To say the least, the venerable and seasoned judge was stunned. He found it very difficult to believe the things he was being told. Was the entire situation a fabrication of Kishen's obsessed mind or was his wishful thinking overtaking reality? At the same time, he also felt that all this could not be concocted, or be just a piece of someone's wild imagination. He also found it strange that Kishen's version matched Rachna's story, and the sequence of events was the same. Rachna had also mentioned that they lived in Chandernagore, next to a river. How her son had disappeared. And how Daataa had planned to bring her child's dead body back to life after seven years of death. Judge Saab was even more intrigued; some shadows seemed to be shaping into reality. He had come across new facts. Perhaps he should extend the judgement date and have the case probed afresh.

And yet, at the same time, the judge wondered if it was possible that Rachna and Kishen had together cooked up this bizarre story. To clear his doubt, Justice Shankar asked Kishen, 'Have you met Rachna?'

'Is she alive? Do you know her? Where is she? Please, I want to meet her, sir! Where is she?' Kishen's excitement was genuine and spontaneous.

Justice Shankar cast aside the little doubt that had arisen

in his mind and replied coolly, 'No, I don't know her and I wonder if she is still alive!'

And in keeping with his strict allegiance to the legal framework, he advised Kishen Das to first go to the police station and tell the concerned police officer about the whole episode. He clarified that Kishen's story was rather unusual and interesting, possibly true, but dealing with past life experiences did not come under the High Court's purview. These stories would have to be substantiated by factual proof and evidence. But, at the same time, based out this story, if further investigations were carried on, then perhaps one could hit upon something worthwhile. Kishen finished the tea and biscuits and having narrated all that had to say, he left.

Justice Shankar kept brooding for a long time after Kishen left. He had never come across such a complex case. On one side there was no eyewitness to confirm allegations, and on the other side, there was the convict's own family, telling nothing but the truth, and yet our legal system would hear none of it! In such a situation, what was a judge to do? It was a terrible, testing time for Justice Shankar. He felt as if his head was placed under a guillotine, and the public was about to pass a harsh verdict on him. But he would still try and hope till the last moment to find the right solution and deliver justice.

Delving deeply into the tussle between facts on one hand and the law on the other, he went into his bedroom to get ready for court. Meera was already there. She saw his bewildered expression and asked him the reason. Justice

Shankar invariably involved Meera in his decision-making whenever he stood at a crossroads. He asked her, 'Suppose there was truth on one side and legal limitations on the other, then who should the judge go with?'

Meera did not hesitate. 'The truth, obviously.'

'That exactly is my problem. Truth tells a different story, but the law will not accept it. The problem is that I need to strike a balance.'

'Is Rachna coming to the court today?' she asked.

'Hmm, let's see. She wants her revenge. But who knows? It will not be easy for her to come to the court. Her life is in danger, you know?'

Meera thought for a while and then said, 'I have a strong intuition that she will. Anyway, you are a judge, and you have to remain within the judicial parameters, so do just what a judge is expected to do. Leave the truth to god.'

As an afterthought she added, 'No one can escape justice from the almighty's court. God has all the facts well chronicled in his register and he himself is an unfaltering eyewitness. Criminals like Daataa Anand may bribe their way out of here, but they cannot lure or cheat god. Daataa will suffer. If nothing else, his own guilty conscience will kill him. And let me tell you, you are not doing any wrong. If the legal procedure and definitions stop you from doing justice, don't take it to heart. You tried your best and you know that. So don't worry, everything will fall in place by god's grace. Have faith.' Meera made it all sound so simple and straight. Her words were like a soothing balm to his troubled mind. He felt light and relieved.

Judge Saab did not know that Meera could come out with solutions just at the snap of a finger. He smiled and hugged her. 'Thank you, my stress-buster, you have eased my tension.'

Exactly at 10 a.m., Justice Shankar sat in his car. He instructed the driver to fill up petrol on the way to the court.

'Sir, the tank is more than half full,' replied the driver, looking at the fuel meter.

'We may not have time in the evening, and tomorrow, early morning, we leave for Calcutta. So do it now,' the judge instructed.

'Okay, sir,' said the driver and they left.

A lot of people had been waiting for this fateful day. Justice Shankar was going to deliver his judgement today. His wife Meera and other family members wanted to get back to their simple life, free from tension and threats. The disciples of Daataa Anand wanted to see him free from all the accusations and were looking forward to just two words in the court—'Not guilty'. The general public wanted to see Daataa chained and given the death sentence. The journalists were waiting to fill their columns with interesting gossip and details. The Emergency was over, but Doordarshan, true to its loyal stance, was still waiting for the orders from the 'high command' to cover the event.

29

Kishen Das was on his way to the police headquarters. He had to meet the officer investigating Daataa's case as suggested by the judge. The time was 10.05 a.m. He stopped over at the petrol pump diagonally opposite Patna High Court. After filling petrol, his car had just about rolled on when he heard a blast. He turned to see what had happened.

A car was in flames, and two old women were running at top speed towards his car. One of them was tall, wore a Tangail saree, and had long, thin, loosely plaited shiny silver hair. Kishen's former vision flashed across his eyes. As if in a trance, he opened the car door. The two women got in and he accelerated away at full speed. He did not understand what had just happened, but his inner self was telling him to help the two poor women. They looked frightened, and one of them said in a shrill, shaky voice, 'Son, quickly take us to the railway station please!'

Without questioning them, without uttering a word, Kishen speeded up towards the station. His mind had stopped functioning, as if the two women had cast a spell on him. He only knew that he had to reach them to the station as fast as he could. All three sat quiet and tense—their muscles stressed and taut, limbs stiff, jaws locked. Every second counted. The only thought on their minds was to just catch hold of any running train and get out of Patna quickly. By the time the police arrived at the petrol pump, the two women had already boarded a running train and left.

The two women looked blissfully relieved once they were on the moving train! Kishen noticed that the other woman, who looked older than the tall one, had both her hands up, as if thanking god for some great good fortune he'd bestowed on them. Immersed in sheer happiness from top to toe, they smiled gleefully at Kishen. Kishen kept staring at them till they went out of sight. As the train whistled out of the station, he suddenly came to his senses and started questioning himself. Who were these two women? Who were they running away from? What had they done? Could they be the ones who had caused the blast? Who was there in that car? Was it right to help them run away like this? Why did he help them?

And yet, at the same time, Kishen felt oddly exhilarated. His mind, heart and conscience supported him wholeheartedly. But what could they have done? They looked innocent. Why was the whole episode disturbing Kishen? He had reacted instinctively and did not regret his decision. Yet, why was he still continuing to think about them? Why was he feeling as if he had just met someone very close to him—his very own mother—and lost her forever without exchanging a single word?

Could they be people from his past life? Could she have been his mother? He had felt so confident that if he ever came face to face with her, he would recognize her at once. Everything about her rang a bell, somewhere in his mind, but could she really have been his mother?

30

There was total chaos at the petrol pump. The people standing there simply froze with shock and fear. They were aghast. No one could make out what had happened. They had vaguely noticed a black Ambassador car standing there. The next moment it had burst into flames following a deafening blast. For a moment the atmosphere had darkened with the flying shards of glass and metal. Gradually, the burnt carcass of the vehicle had settled down, its inmates also a charred part of the mangled heap. The number plate was thrown aside, with one visible number, zero—a pitiable reminder of transient life.

Whose car had it been? Who had been sitting inside it? The police was trying to decipher the mess. Meanwhile, a battalion of onlookers had suddenly discovered their purpose for the day—they stood there wondering what had happened!

Five minutes later, when Justice Shankar was crossing that road, it was jammed. His driver got down and found out that an extremely unfortunate accident had taken place. Someone's car was badly devastated in a fire, probably due to a bomb blast. Nobody knew whose car it was, or who were sitting in it. Whoever it was, was dead and charred beyond recognition. How it had happened was also a mystery! No one had seen or noticed anything odd or out of the ordinary during the whole incident.

Meanwhile, Justice Shankar was totally ignorant of the fact that Rachna was going to wait for him at that particular petrol pump that very day. No one had informed him that he was supposed to pick her up from there. Or for that matter that she was going to create a sensation in the court by folly exposing Daataa Anand's criminal pursuits. Or that she would be the witness for the prosecution. Nothing like this was ever finalized or even mentioned to him. He was unaware of all the plots and susplots, and was following his normal routine. Rachna was on his mind, and he would have liked her to come to court, but he very much doubted her attendance.

Some people had seen two beggar-women running away from the ill-fated car. That was but natural—anyone would have tried to save his or her life; there was nothing unusual in that. And after the blast, no one even tried to see where those two insignificant old women were going or what they were doing. Their gaze was fixed on the burning car. Nobody noticed them fleeing from there.

31

What had happened was this: Daataa Anand had instructed his lieutenants to reach the court directly and not to wait for him. They had reached well on time and were asking each other if they had any further instructions. It was so unlike Daataa not to come on time. They all remembered Daataa's lectures on punctuality. What had happened today? Where was he held up? And if he had some other appointment, then why had he not informed them that he would be late?

Even his armed guards were all in the court. This was so unusual that they looked at each other and expressed concern. 'If all of us are here, then who was accompanying Daataa? Where had he gone alone?'

The ragpicker staying at his ashram had painted such dismal pictures, manoeuvred his emotions, and had taken advantage of his vulnerability in such a way that Daataa had no options left. She told him that everyone recognized his car and Rachna would run away the moment she saw it. Daataa was highly impressed with her far-sightedness. He thought that the old woman was absolutely right in pointing this out to him. Immediately, he got his people to organize an unidentified car. He did not tell any of his close aides about his plans. He did not want his followers to know about Rachna. He wanted to keep the dirt in his backyard hidden from the world. They must not see or know the real him.

How the mighty fall when fate intervenes! He had executed any number of deaths without batting an eyelid. The poor souls had to die because Daataa valued his secrets much more than an ordinary human life! But today, he was whimpering for his own life. He was scared like a little mouse. Rachna knew so much about him, she could undo all that he had done so far. Her statements could easily take him to the gallows. He was terribly shaken and scared. He could see his life coming to an end and he was ready to do anything that could save him. Quietly, he agreed to all the terms and conditions that the beggar-woman had put. His life was now in her hands, and he was following her meekly, like a frightened lamb about to be slaughtered.

Many of his followers had seen the black Ambassador car at the petrol pump, but little did they know that their guru was sitting inside. They were all on their way to the High Court. There was no one to keep an eye on the two old ragpickers.

If Daataa had had the slightest doubt, he would have called his bodyguards. But he was so anxious to save his own life and his secrets that he could see nothing beyond his saviour. So paranoid was he that even when the car caught fire, he did not open the door and rush out, because his eyes were fixed on Rachna running away from him.

When Daataa first saw Rachna coming towards his car, his 'angel', the old woman, was standing outside. He did not see that the woman had the petrol tank's cover in her hand and that a bunch of lighted matches was in Rachna's hands. The bomb had been planted in the dickey of the car in the morning itself, inside the ragpicker's sack, the same sack which she had been carrying with her the day she first met Daataa. The bomb had been in the sack at that time also, but those days, life was much simpler—people had mutual trust, and security checks were not mandatory at places like an ashram.

Rachna opened the door of the black Ambassador with one hand, dropped the burning matches in the petrol tank with her other hand, looked at Daataa, smiled, and ran away. All this happened in a flash. Daataa thought she was running away from him and he shouted, 'Catch her, catch her!' The beggar-woman ran after her. Daataa was too busy looking at the two women running, one trying to catch the other.

He failed to notice the fire.

One blast—and the car jumped up four feet above the ground. Another blast, and the car was ripped apart. It was then quickly engulfed by flames.

It took less than half a second for Daataa Anand's world to end. Even a spiritual guru had no control over anything.

Ultimately, he, too, was mortal like his followers. The special power that he had acquired over the years with deep meditation and various other ways did nothing to help him. Life and death were never his for the taking.

32

The court was fully packed. Journalists, cameramen, disciples, the general public, were all loitering around in the corridors. But when the time allotted for the case ran out and Daataa did not turn up, people were surprised. Everyone thought that Daataa had gone underground, thinking that the judgement would go against him. People were also discussing the bomb blast at the petrol pump. The rumours everyone had heard was that the fire brigade had not arrived on time and the bodies had charred beyond identification.

Justice Shankar and Justice Mukherjee took their seats in the court. The counsel for defence had made a special request to the bench to wait for Daataa Anand. But when he did not arrive at the end of the stipulated time, the judgement was reserved for a later date. However, a contempt-of-court charge was levelled against Daataa, and a warrant of arrest issued against his name. The next date would be announced when the court reopened after Diwali. The court was then adjourned.

Meera had already started feeling relieved. She was very happy that that day the various tensions and fears that were plaguing her family would finally come to an end. She had began planning a family holiday. Time was ticking extremely slowly as Meera waited for her husband to come back home. She couldn't wait to hear the final verdict. And whatever the verdict was, she knew that she would celebrate Diwali with many more diyas and fireworks than usual this time, and would offer a special puja to Lord Ganesh and the goddess Laxmi, and distribute sweets to everyone.

33

Daataa Anand's ashram too wore a festive look that day. They were waiting for him to finally shake off all the charges that had been wrongly levelled against him. They knew that the court could not have found him guilty. His innocence had been proved beyond doubt. It was just a matter of hours before he would be home, a free and happy man. They were all going to celebrate his victory together.

A havan was being performed, the ashram adorned with fresh flowers and marigold garlands. They knew that today their revered guru Daataa Anand would also join them in singing and dancing. Ecstasy was in the air. His ardent followers had already started swinging with joy. The ashram reverberated with non-stop singing:

Anandam hi anandam, le anandam de anandam
Daataa bole kshanik janam, anandam hi anandam.

If the only knew what had happened! They had no clue about how Daataa's soul must have suffered the agony of being burnt alive. His own cruelty to others had boomeranged back at him. God had made him go through the same unbearable, excruciating pain that he had meted out to his followers. He had been made to realize the barbarity of his own beastly acts. Perhaps now his soul would repent and atone for the sins he had committed! Justice had been carried out and the culprit had been punished even before the court had fixed another date for judgement. Meera had been right when she had told her husband to follow the judicial parameters and leave justice to god.

The almighty did not need witnesses to find the truth—he already knew the facts, and Daataa's tribe had not been able to intimidate or bribe him.

A FEW YEARS LATER

Daataa Anand's disciples still hoped that one day their guru would come back to them. They believed that he had probably gone on some spiritual journey to the Himalayas, perhaps in disguise. Every now and then some of the more optimist devotees sang and danced but soon the tempo slowed and the exuberance vanished.

The Emergency survived in the memory of people, and now they could openly question the motive behind its enforcement. The government that came into being after the elections wanted to honour Justice Shankar for his bravery and sense of fairness during the Emergency. They said, 'At a time when even the Supreme Court's judgments were questionable, the Hon'ble judge exhibited exemplary courage by showing allegiance to the constitution and upholding civil liberties, thus safeguarding democracy. For this he deserves to be felicitated.' Justice Shankar gracefully refused the honour, saying that he had only been doing his duty.

Justice Shankar never came to know about Rachna's devastatingly simple and brilliant move. And he never realized he had been an unwitting participant in her scheme to punish Daataa Anand. The judge never did find out how Rachna and her friend had set the trap for Daataa. How Daataa was tricked into believing the beggar woman. How he had come to the petrol pump just to meet Rachna, little realizing the danger to his life, and how she had avenged her dead son and pronounced the final judgement on Daataa Anand in no uncertain terms!

Rachna had meticulously planned all the details of her revenge, right up to the time that Daataa Anand's car was to be blown up. It had seemed such an impossible task that she had not thought out what they would do if they succeeded. Instead, they had prepared themselves to bravely face consequences if they were caught. The sole focus was that Daataa should be punished. Under no circumstances was he to go free. 'Declared innocent and honourably acquitted', was the one sentence that would have been like a tight slap on the face of entire mankind and humanity, it would be an abuse of society, a corruption of the highest order and a public shaming of the judiciary. Also, Rachna would never have been able to forgive herself if she had not taken revenge for her son's inhuman torture and death. And at the end of it all, Rachna had no regrets for what she had done with the help of her very trustworthy and sincere friend.

However, much later, Rachna often found herself remembering the young boy who had helped them run away. She thought to herself, he was truly sent by god. How fast he drove to reach us to the station! How sweetly he helped us climb on to the running train! How he kept looking at me with those beautiful, innocent eyes! He seemed to have such a connection to me, as if he were my own flesh and blood. How I felt like hugging him, cuddling him, slipping my fingers through his hair. If only I could see him again!

Kishen Das was now free from his mysterious ailment. His life was one happy sojourn with his wife Seema. They had a cute little cottage with a small garden in Secunderabad. Mr Das's ambition, however, remained unfulfilled as Kishen refused to sit for the entrance exam for the civil services and opted instead for a job in the private sector. While they agreed on certain things, like the faults of the government in power, their verbal duels continued. That was the only way the two could express affection for each other. A new addition in this sparring was Seema, who took up the position of referee.

Kishen's engagement with his previous birth was a thing that was firmly in the past. However, once in a while, the face of the woman he had helped flashed in his mind. How she had come running for her very life to his car. He remembered the beautiful face, her long, loosely plaited silver hair. He tried to recollect if she was wearing a coin-sized red bindi on her forehead but for the life of him could not remember. God only knew where she had gone or where she was now. Was she alive still, or gone forever? Kishen Das still harboured the faint hope that perhaps one day their paths would cross.

There was definitely something very special about that, face. The moment Kishen would think of her, the child in him would come alive. He felt as if someone was stroking his hair softly, affectionately. He wanted to believe that the woman he had helped to run away, whose life he had perhaps saved, was none other than his mother, Rachna, and that he was her shonamun. And, like any little child, he thirsted to meet his mother, to touch her and to hug her. But would he ever be able to find her? Perhaps in another destiny, another life!

ACKNOWLEDGEMENTS

A very special thank you to Sanjita Sinha for all the help and support. I would also like to thank Ms Anita Karwal for sharing her experiences of regressive hypnosis therapy with me and Mr Prashant Vedsen for providing factual information regarding the case. I would like to thank Mr A.A. Sahay, Mr J.L. Mehta, Ms Kumud Mehta, Mr Deepak Sinha, Ms Kusum Sinha, Ms Madhu Varma, Ms Gunjan Bahadur, Ms Rama Sinha, Mr G.S. Dutt and Ms Shibani Goyal for reading the manuscript at various stages and providing invaluable help with it. And last, but not the least, my heartfelt thanks to Sunit, Shalini, Pratyush and Teeshna for encouraging me to approach publishers and to Penguin for publishing *The Dance of Death*.

Read more in Penguin

CAN LOVE HAPPEN TWICE?
Ravinder Singh

When Ravin first said 'I love you . . .' he meant it forever. The world has known this through Ravin's bestselling novel, *I Too Had a Love Story*. But did Ravin's story really end on the last page of that book?

On Valentine's Day, a radio station in Chandigarh hosts a very special romantic chat show. Ravin and his three best friends are invited as guests to talk about Ravin's love story. But surprisingly everyone apart from Ravin turns up. As the show goes live, there is only one question in every listener's mind: what has happened to Ravin?

To answer this question the three friends begin reading from a handwritten copy of Ravin's incomplete second book—the entire city listens breathlessly, unable to believe the revelations that follow.

Penguin Books India
Fiction
INR 125

Read more in Penguin

I NEVER THOUGHT I COULD FALL IN LOVE
Chanchaldeep Singh Sandhu

Could life *be* any better?

Playboy Ronnie thinks he has hit the jackpot when he has sex with Miss Fresher in her car on Freshers' Night; saves himself from ragging by making fools of his seniors; and when his money-making scheme with his friend promises to bring in the much-needed moolah for having fun!

But destiny seems to have its own plans and soon Ronnie falls in love! However, the journey from lust to love is not easy. Fighting his playboy image, and his best friend, Mickey, Ronnie has to now convince the girl of his dreams that 'she is the only one for him'. Even if it means almost getting killed by a criminal gang and breaking into the girls' hostel to declare his love!

I Never Thought I Could Fall in Love is a racy, naughty and heart-warming love-story of a boy who did not know what he was capable of doing in life until he fell in love.

Penguin Books India
Fiction
INR 99